———————— ★ ————————

We made our way carefully across the site, finding it hard to see in the growing darkness. I saw that a worker had left a toolbox there, and a jacket lying on the ground. I blinked in the dark as I slowly, unwillingly, realized there was a hand in the jacket sleeve. I gasped, and Vera, right behind me, saw where I was looking.

We were down on our knees in the mud, checking for a pulse, checking for a breath, starting CPR.

"Kay, can you do this?"

I whispered, "Yes," and stepped into the rhythms of Vera's chest pressure as she said, "I'm calling 911." She ran off, cursing, while I kept up the breathing and pressure until she returned and took over again. We couldn't stop, but we both had known, from the moment we touched him, that he was dead.

———————— ★ ————————

"I loved Triss Stein's new story. It has everything: a resourceful heroine, ancient crimes, modern crimes, lots of New York color, and a breathtaking finish."

—Janet Evanovich

Previously published Worldwide Mystery title by
TRISS STEIN

MURDER AT THE CLASS REUNION

DIGGING UP
DEATH

TRISS STEIN

WORLDWIDE.

TORONTO • NEW YORK • LONDON
AMSTERDAM • PARIS • SYDNEY • HAMBURG
STOCKHOLM • ATHENS • TOKYO • MILAN
MADRID • WARSAW • BUDAPEST • AUCKLAND

With love, to Bob, Miriam and Carolyn,
who keep my life interesting

DIGGING UP DEATH

A Worldwide Mystery/May 1999

Published by arrangement with Walker Publishing Company, Inc.

ISBN 0-373-26310-4

Acknowledgments

This book could not have been written without the help of experts. Any mistakes and improbabilities are my own. My thanks to the fine writers and astute but gentle critics in my writing circle—Peggy Ehrhart, Phyllis Halterman, Barbara Robinson, and Madeline Weitsman; to archaeologists Nan Rothschild, of Barnard College, who generously answered questions over the past few years; to Diana Wall, of City College, who helped me get started, and Celia Bergoffen, who taught a great class on New York City archaeology at New York University; and to my friend, attorney Andrea Kremen, who shared her real-estate development expertise.

Author's Note

The tavern in this story, and its owner, are entirely fictitious, but Captain Kidd was, of course, a real historical figure. I couldn't begin to use all the fascinating information I found about him, about pirates in old New York, and about the early city itself. Especially valuable sources were Robert C. Ritchie's *Captain Kidd and the War Against the Pirates* (Harvard University Press, 1986) and Thomas Archdeacon's *New York City, 1664-1710: Conquest and Change* (Cornell University Press, 1976). The quote on page 22 is accurate and comes from Nan Rothschild's book, *New York City Neighborhoods: The Eighteenth Century* (Academic Press, 1990).

PROLOGUE

HE GRIPPED THE TORCH in his hand and stood in the shadows of another building, watching with hatred as the merrymakers went in and out. He touched the gold coin he wore on a thong around his neck. For luck. It was all he had left. The land was his. The building was his. His stolen money had built it. He wanted it back.

From time to time he could glimpse the outline of a plumed hat or a raised tankard at a window. The door would open, and there would be a burst of laughter; loud, sociable talk; snatches of a bawdy song. What did he care for them? He cared only about regaining what was his. Or revenge. At last he blew on the torch until the flames blazed up, then threw it, following its arc until it landed on the dry thatch roof.

He stood under the trees, watching, as the first man leaving the tavern smelled the smoke, looked up to the burning roof, and gave the dreaded cry, "Fire!" It was a very old building for this new world, wood frame, put up before most of the new brick buildings. It would burn quickly.

The merrymakers in the tavern rushed out in a stampede of fear. His enemy came out too, directed men to the water buckets, and then went back in, into the already spreading fire.

The man under the trees knew why. Somewhere inside was what belonged to him. Perhaps in a strongbox, or a leathern bag, perhaps hidden under a cellar paving stone. There would be a handful of gold and silver coins, Spanish and Dutch, and some with unknown markings that had traveled half around the world, by trade and capture, from who knows where. Perhaps some trinkets too, a few loose gems, and some good weapons lifted from dead sailors who had sailed under other flags. The leavings after his enemy had bought land and a home and a safe livelihood away from the sea. Not a chestful of treasure, but more than enough for a poor man to brave a fire.

They had been friends once. Or comrades at least. Shared the joy of hoisted sails billowing, with the ship running before a fair wind. The despair of calm seas, with dead air and provisions running low. The strangeness of places where the air smelled of spices, the dark-skinned men wore gowns like women, and the women wore veils that tantalized as they concealed. They had followed their captain into the whirlwind, those terrifying and glorious moments when they hurled themselves aboard another ship and claimed her for their own.

But all that had died during the long years ashore, when his old comrade had prospered and he had lost everything, and lawsuits and threats had brought no satisfaction. No. This was not the shipmate whose back he'd covered in fights with the cursed Spanish. No, this was his enemy. He felt now as if he were boarding a Spanish ship one last time. He'd faced death a score of times, cheated the reaper three or four. He would prevail and claim his prize at last.

And he moved toward the building, to follow his enemy and take from him what was his. In the dark and confusion no one noticed the man in rough clothes pushing his way toward the fire. No one saw the gleam of the coin he wore at his neck nor the glow of madness in his face.

Within, the man who owned the tavern hurried down to the cellar, desperate to save the two items of value he had hidden there. At his belt he had his dagger, to prize up the loose stone that hid his money, and in his hand he had a key, to unlock the valuable slave he had just acquired in payment for a debt. Would the man run if let loose? Perhaps, but burned to a cinder he would be worthless. Better to take a chance on a runaway. He wouldn't get far, fresh from Madagascar as he was, without clothes or money or a language anyone hereabouts could understand.

He was kneeling over the paving stones, working the knife point around the loose one, when an arm went around his neck, and he smelled whiskey-soaked breath and heard a familiar whiskey-soaked voice muttering in his ear. He tensed, gathered his strength, and reared back sharply. His assailant, caught off guard, loosed his hold and fell, dragging the other man down on top of him. They rolled on the floor, flailing and punching and gouging, and all the time the cellar was slowly filling with smoke. One man was healthy, well-fed, and strong, and knew he was fighting for his life. The other was drunk and ill, but propelled by rage and long-cherished resentment. They were well matched.

The weaker of the two was winning, sitting on his enemy's chest, hands clenched around his neck, pounding his head against the stone floor. The man on the floor was close to losing consciousness, but his groping hand reached the dagger he had dropped. And he drove it home.

He staggered to his feet. He was all but passing out from the smoke. He made his way blindly toward the stairs, his only thought a desperate, instinctive search for air. He forgot about the coins hidden under the stones. And he forgot about the slave, hidden in the cellar's back room, shackled to the wall.

Deep in the basement, the African smelled the smoke. He did not know the English words for *fire* or *help,* and he did not know the Dutch words, but he knew what fire was, and he knew what chains were. He pulled at them, again and again, but even in his fear and anger he was not strong enough to rip them from the wall. He shouted in his own language, in the hope that someone would at least hear his voice. And as the smoke began to overcome him, he prayed to his own gods, as he had prayed every day during the long nightmare voyage: to send him home to his own people.

As the flames raged, the neighbors rallied around with buckets, driven by the terror of spreading fire, but they could not save the old wooden building. It soon collapsed in upon itself and burned to the ground. When there was nothing left but charred timbers and the reek of smoke, they found the man who had owned the tavern. He had collapsed just inside what had been the front door. They carried him out, gently, and brought him home to his widow.

In time, the burned rubble on the surface was cleared. They used it to fill in the hole where the basement used to be. They filled it in with earth and put up a new building, fire-resistant brick and tile, as the new fire laws demanded.

Over the years the new little building became another tavern, a greengrocer, a hat maker. In time, it was replaced by a row of tenements. Gas lights were put in, the streets were repaved and straightened, and that end of the block was cut off from the main avenues. Even as the neighborhood grew up around it, into the greatest financial center in the world, that little corner of the great city remained untouched and obscure.

The basement kept its secrets.

ONE

"KAY! I'm glad you're back," Vera was saying on the phone. "Your office told me you were on assignment, and then I got too busy to call…"

"I've been back a few weeks. Are you in town for a while? You sound excited."

"You bet I'm excited. You've got to come and see what I'm working on. When can you come? Today?"

"Why? What's up? Are you at Barnard?"

"Nope, not for the summer, and only part-time next semester. Kay, can you believe it? I'm directing my own dig. Finally."

"Congratulations! You've earned it."

"I sure have. It should have happened years ago, but I might've lucked out on this one. So, can you come see?"

"I'll come, but where are you? Please say it's not some fort in the Adirondack backwoods, fifty miles from a paved road."

She giggled. "Try fifty feet from Wall Street. So just hustle yourself into a cab and get down here. I won't tell you a thing till you do. Not a word."

I knew she meant it, and I thought, Why not? I had nothing pressing to do, and of course my curiosity was stirred. Of course, Vera knew it would be.

"Okay, okay, I'm out the door. Just give me the address and stick around until I get there."

So there I was, sitting in a cab stuck in downtown traffic, thinking about my friend Vera.

Vera was the friend I could trust forever. We go back almost twenty years, all the way back to the first week of our first year at college, when we were newly hatched into adulthood and barely fledged. In those days Vera still used a cute giggle and accent to disguise her serious scholarliness, and I was still pretending that ambition and brains could substitute for friends.

Vera was probably fated to become an archaeologist. In every dorm room we shared, she'd had a quotation from Mary Renault tacked to the bulletin board. It read, "We shall never know ourselves until we have taken a long look back along the rocky road which brought us where we are." I wasn't convinced. I lived most of my life in the present and immediate future, a journalist working from today's deadline to tomorrow's.

When I left daily journalism for a more stable job on a magazine in New York, and she landed a teaching job at Barnard, we were able to see each other regularly. Still, we'd both been busy in the last few months. I had recently returned from my unexpectedly eventful twentieth high-school reunion, way upstate, and I had a lot to tell her. It turned out she had a lot to tell me too.

The cabdriver got lost several times in the twisty maze of the financial district streets, but we finally pulled up at a huge construction site, a block square. A big sign said Elkan Properties. I circled the temporary wooden wall that surrounded the site, finally finding the way in, but a middle-aged man in a hard hat stopped me.

"Excuse me, miss, you can't come on the building site. The public can look through the openings we cut in the wall," he said, pointing to one.

I almost said, "Hey, I'm not public, I'm press," but I knew it was more to the point to just respond, "I was invited. There's an archaeologist here named Vera Contas...."

"Vera? Oh, sure, she's over there. Here, take a hard hat, and walk careful. It's muddy from the rain, ya know. You'll probably find her down in the pit."

That's exactly where she was, working in a small dug-out area at the edge of the noise and controlled chaos of a major construction site.

"Kay!" she shouted. "I'll be right up."

I was always impressed by how little Vera seemed to change. Her life kept her fit and slim, the same petite girl I'd met on my freshman floor. Her blond hair hid any gray she may have developed, and her lipstick was in place no matter how much mud was on her clothes. In fact, she managed to look cute even in her muddy work clothes. I envied that; my style leans more toward elegance, but I have to work at it.

She scrambled up the sloping side of the pit, took me by the arm, and led me into a very small, cluttered shed. Her desk was just a cheap card table, piled with ancient-looking maps and grid paper marked out in colored pencils.

"My office," she said grandly. "What do you think?"

She saw my face and laughed. "Okay, it's small, dark, and a mess, but besides that? It's the first time I've ever had a field office."

"Vera, enough mystery. What's going on here?"

"I've been hired by Elkan to do a preliminary archaeological survey. It's part of the deal when they ask for a building variance. You have to love a law that provides work for impoverished archaeologists. So I've been cultivating the guys at Landmarks Preservation, and they finally recommended me."

"Doesn't this usually happen before they start building?" I gestured toward the loud activity outside.

"Yes, sure, but this time they'd started the building on *that* site, not being able to buy *this* piece of land. Then suddenly they could get it. Someone died, I think, and the heirs were ready to deal.

They're adding a wing or plaza or some damn thing. Naturally, they'd like me to decide there's nothing here, finish up, and get the hell out, but"— she lowered her voice—"I think we're onto something here, and I have to admit, Elkan himself has been somewhat supportive."

With the construction noise outside, no one could possibly have heard her, and I told her so. Her secrecy seemed ridiculous, and also surprising. Vera will usually tell anything, her own secrets or someone else's.

Her only response was "It will be quiet in a few minutes. It's almost quitting time for these guys. Then I can show you around without anyone listening or watching."

The noise stopped suddenly when a whistle blew. "Now you can hear me. Come take a look."

On a rickety shelf and in baskets there were round, flat-bottomed bottles that looked like brown pottery but sounded like glass when I tapped with my nail; pieces of white clay pipes; a shiny earthenware jug, put together from fragments; and a dish of ceramic and stone marbles.

"All right, Vera, I give up. What does it all mean?"

"Those marbles are gaming pieces, and these are wine bottles." She touched the flat-bottomed, brown ones. "They're glass. They were green then, back when Peter Stuyvesant might have had a drink from one. Think about it, Kay. You're holding a piece of history, something you can touch from the days when New York was a mile long, and the wall on Wall Street kept the wild animals out.'' She went on, ''We're finding lots of pipes. The Dutch were smokers, and there were plenty of them left even after the English took over.

''Now, this type of jug was used for serving beer. Kay, this was a tavern; I'm sure of *that;* and it wasn't just any old saloon.'' Her eyes were sparkling, and she dropped her voice to a whisper again.

''If I say it was a sea captain's hangout, and some of those captains were just basically pirates; that there was a connection to Captain Kidd himself; that I'd bet big money—well, I *am* betting my career—that what we're going to find would be front-page news...''

''Vera, what the *hell* are you getting at?''

She shook her head and grinned. ''Can't say yet, even to you. I have to dig up more physical evidence to prove it, because it's so hard to match those seventeenth-century maps to the real city out there. Their city just disappeared a long time ago.'' She was pointing to places on the quaint map spread out on her desk.

''Hills were leveled, streams paved over, streets just vanished. But,'' she finished with another grin, ''ask me again in a couple of days. I'm so sure, I'll bet you dinner anywhere in the city, your choice.''

As irritated as I was by Vera's mysterious act, I could see that if this site was as important as she thought, it would be the making of her career at last. There was only one thing for me to say, and I said it.

"If it's that big, I want the story! Exclusively, all the juicy details, everything. As soon as you really know and way before anyone else. Promise?"

"Of course, of course."

"In that case, let's go celebrate. My treat."

"You're on! Just walk with me over to that office building across the street, will you? I've made friends with the guard. He lets me use a rest room to clean up and change, bless him. After digging all day, I'm too foul to be out in public." As we walked, she added, with a laugh, "When I go straight home after work, I find people kind of edging away from me in the subway."

She said a cheery good-night to the man who'd let me in and added, "Jerry, have they made you the night guard along with everything else? Project supervisor isn't enough?"

He smiled indulgently. "Naw, he'll be along soon, but you know the buck stops with me. I'm just making sure everything's shut down like it oughta be. Some of the younger guys have been a little careless lately. See you tomorrow, Vera."

VERA CHANGED, and we walked out into the eerie quiet of the financial district after hours. It never really shuts down, but the flood of cars and cabs diminishes to a trickle, and the noise dies down to a hum. The narrow streets twisted as they had when Vera's sea captains drank at the tavern she thought she'd found, and on certain blocks, the harbor, with seagulls wheeling in the pale, wide-open sky above it, could be glimpsed suddenly between the skyscrapers. We went into a bar packed with Wall Street types, traders just as the old captains had been, only now they traded stocks and bonds by computer, instead of beaver skins and slaves by ship.

Vera made a face at the pin-striped crowd. "No avoiding them around here at this hour, and anyway the burgers are good."

She talked in a breathless rush about her hopes for the dig, and moaned about how long this had been in coming.

"Well, if you hadn't dropped out of graduate school to follow that guy around the country picking up jobs at digs wherever you could—"

"Shovel bumming! Don't remind me! But it was fun, and worth it too, while it lasted." She made a face. "Who could know he would turn out to be such a creep? Oh well, that was years ago, and grad school was still there when I got back."

"Anything interesting going on in your social

life these days? I can't believe it's been a couple
of months since we've talked.''

She said slowly, ''No, not a damn thing. I'm living for work. Incredible, isn't it? But I just don't
have the time for that kind of distraction right
now.'' She saw my skeptical look, turned red, and
insisted, ''No, I mean it this time.''

I smiled.

''Oh, stop, Kay. I do! Now, tell me what you've
been up to.''

I told it all in my best storytelling fashion, turning my near-panic at a reunion with high school
classmates, in the hometown where I'd been so unhappy, into a funny story. The discovery of a body
at the party didn't need any dramatic help from me,
and the whole story of the murder kept me going
until dessert. But I didn't tell even Vera about
Tony, my old friend and new lover. And I didn't
tell her what I'd learned about my parents.

''Anyway,'' I wound up, ''my hometown turned
out to be more interesting than I expected, and I
might even go back for an extended trip—write a
book if I can, about changing small-town life. Now,
don't say I'll shrivel up and die away from New
York. I've heard enough of that!''

She laughed. ''Not me! If it has hot showers and
a daily paper, I think it's the height of civilization.
I was once on a site way up in the Catskills where

I swear it was ten miles to the nearest indoor plumbing.

"Let's get going," she added, signaling the waiter. "I need to pick up some things back at the site, and my muscles are screaming for a hot bath."

It was still the long summer evening, not quite dark but not bright enough to see much. I could hear the ferries' deep signals from the harbor. We carefully negotiated our way across broken pavement and around construction barriers, and Vera said, "I read a description the other day of New York streets as 'nasty and unregarded, due to the pace of building.' When do you think it was written?"

"Last year? Last decade?"

"1697," she said smugly. "Some things about this city never change."

At the site there was no watchman, but Vera had her own key to the padlocked gate. We went in, sidestepping puddles as we walked across the property to her office. I waited outside the shed and looked up at the darkening sky and the bands of lights going on and off in the office towers as night workers moved through the buildings.

She came out and said, "I'm ready. We can find transportation over that way a block or two. Maybe if we walk to the gate along here, closer to the fence, we can avoid some of that mud."

We made our way carefully across the site, finding it hard to see in the growing darkness. I tripped painfully and caught myself on a stack of lumber, leaning against it to check my ankle for a sprain. I saw that a worker had left a toolbox there, and a jacket lying on the ground. I blinked in the dark as I slowly, unwillingly, realized there was a hand in the jacket sleeve. I gasped, and Vera, right behind me, saw where I was looking.

It all happened in a second that seemed to last an hour. We were down on our knees in the mud, checking for a pulse, checking for a breath, starting CPR.

"Kay, can you do this?"

I whispered, "Yes," and stepped into the rhythms of Vera's chest pressure as she said, "I'm calling 911. Shit." She ran off, cursing, while I kept up the breathing and pressure until she returned and took over again. We couldn't stop, but we both had known, from the moment we touched him, that he was dead.

TWO

THE NIGHT SEEMED to last forever. The Emergency Medical Service crew worked for a long time, only to confirm in the end what we already knew. The police arrived and asked a few questions, took our names and phone numbers.

I watched as they checked his wallet for ID. It was all there: driver's license, union card, video store membership, health plan card. He was a construction worker on the site, and he was all of twenty-four years old.

I watched as they shone their flashlights over the dead man while the ambulance crew pointed out the wound at the back of his head. They walked around, moving the lights so they skimmed every nearby surface. I watched as one of them beckoned the other to look at the sharp edge of a pile of metal pipes near where the young man was lying. There was a bloody spot there, deep gouges in the mud, and matching muddy streaks on his back. I moved close enough to hear one of the cops say, "Must've slipped, poor bastard. Looks like he hit his head right here."

"Drunk, maybe." More like probably than maybe. He reeked of beer. "Kay," Vera was saying, "do you want to go home? They've called the construction company manager and the owner, and I should stick around to see them, but you've done everything you need to."

"Yes," I said. "I should go home. I have work tomorrow, starting with an early meeting. If anything happens later, you'll tell me?" Vera agreed, and I started to leave, only to turn back. "Did you know him?"

She nodded. "A little. His name is—was—Kevin. He'd stop by sometimes to ask me about what we were doing. He even found interesting little things on his own a couple of times and brought them to me. He was like a big, curious kid...." Her voice wavered, and she rubbed a muddy hand across her eyes.

"Are you okay?"

"Me? Yeah, just tired. At least I don't have to call his family, his boss will do that." She seemed to sag, and steadied herself against a fence, but she waved her hand at me. "Go on. Go home."

"I'm going. Be in touch tomorrow, okay?"

It felt unnatural not to be doing something, taking notes, asking questions, writing a story—but this time I was only a bystander. This wasn't a story. The accidental death of an unknown worker in a moderately dangerous occupation was not a news story. No one would care except those who loved him.

When I got home, I fought down the impulse to call Tony. It was much too late, but even more, I was uncomfortable with the thought of turning to him that way. I'd been on my own for a long time, and I wasn't ready to rely on him, or anyone. Was I?

He was a friend, of sorts, from my adolescence. We'd met again at my reunion and begun what was not quite a romance, knowing, when I left, that it would continue. A week later he came to New York on business, and though he had a hotel reservation, I think we both knew he would stay with me. We had our first real date in normal circumstances and two of the best nights of my life.

When he was getting ready to leave, we tried to joke about rendezvousing in Albany, but in the end, saying good-bye was astonishingly difficult.

"We know now, don't we?" he had said. "It can't be just a fling, can it?"

"No," I said. "I wish it could."

"We'll find a way. The only problems are distance and work and my kids." He smiled a little. "Nothing serious."

He hugged me and left, finally, not really understanding that I meant I wished it *could* be just a fling. I didn't want to feel about anyone what I was starting to feel about Tony. I was standing at the top of a slippery slope, on waxed skis, digging in my poles, trying hard not to start down.

So I didn't call him. In the end I was so tired, I managed to stay awake just long enough to switch on the air conditioner and change into a nightshirt. I fell asleep even before I turned off my light, but all night long, in my dreams, I saw that pale, mud-streaked young face in the bright beam of the cop's flashlight. I woke up thinking, not for the first time, that I was getting too old and too soft for this reporting racket.

The next morning, my boss was having none of it.

"This is the best job in journalism, Kay."

"I know it, Howard." Well, one of the best, I thought. "But I'm tired and stale. I need a break."

"You? Stale? You gave us a great series on your reunion. Great stuff. You've done two first-class interviews since you got back. You can't be serious about this small-town book. No one would read it. Who cares? And you'd hate living there; you'd be bored to death in no time."

"You aren't listening, Howard. Do I have to fax you the message? I could *use* a little boredom!"

He looked at me with disbelief. "See what I mean? A month in the country, and your brain is growing moss." Before I answered as angrily as I wanted to, he went on quietly, "Kay, I've been in journalism thirty-five years, and maybe half of the journalists I've known wanted to write a book. You know how many ever did? Okay, I don't know either, but not many. You get addicted to the pressure, and your brains die without it.''

I was probably turning red, because he said, ''Okay, okay, how about this? You've only been back a few weeks. Give yourself a few more. Get acclimated. Ease back into the routine. Then we'll talk again in, say, a month.''

''Oh, all right,'' I said, ''but I'm not going to change my mind.'' I wasn't, I was sure of that, but I wasn't ready to just quit on the spot.

''We'll see. In the meantime, we've got a follow-up on that story from last month, about the mayor from Indiana who's under indictment, and he will only talk to you. Travel has your ticket to Indianapolis.''

''You call this 'easing in?'''

''Kay, it's only a couple of days. Come on! And you say you *like* small towns now, so this should be just right for you.'' I could swear I heard a chuckle. Nothing makes me angrier than feeling I'm not being taken seriously.

''By the way, Kay, any special reason you were late this morning, and look like you were up half the night? You don't have that exhausted but happy, I-caroused-all-night look.''

I told him, and he said, ''You're right; there's no story there. Archaeology isn't exactly Princess Di, when it comes to selling magazines. I need something dramatic: bones, conflict. Buried treasure would be good.... And the accident is not news.''

"Howard, I wonder about that. I have all these little questions. I mean, I know there's nothing to pitch as a story, not yet, but something feels funny about it.''

He thought it over. "You've got nothing but a feeling?" He shook his head, then said, "What the hell. These feelings have been known to pay off. I don't mind if you keep a little eye on it when you get back. Call it company time, as long as you don't take much of it. Poke in the mud and hang out with your friend.''

Before I could say anything, he added, "I know, I'm great and thoughtful and it's barely compensation for sending you back to Indiana and putting you off on the leave. No need to thank me. Just trying to keep the help happy.''

He waved me out and picked up his phone. Impulsive thoughtfulness wasn't the way Howard normally ran the department. I wondered with some satisfaction if my desire to leave the magazine had scared him.

A few days later, when I got home from Indiana, I tried to call Vera, but I kept missing her. I finally decided the only solution was to visit her at the site.

She wasn't in her makeshift office, but there were a few workers around who pointed me to the large and substantial trailer that served as the main construction office.

Vera was there, surprisingly dressed in business clothes, and with her was a man in a dark suit. In the moment when he turned to be introduced, I had a fleeting impression that he was well dressed, in the subtle, perfectly-tailored-suit, discreet-silk-tie style of a wealthy banker. Then Vera was introducing him as Alan Elkan, and I was looking at a very attractive man. I suddenly wished I'd checked my hair and makeup.

When he shook my hand he said, "It's a pleasure to meet you. I've admired some of your pieces in *News Now*. Is this a social visit, or is there news here I don't know about?"

"Strictly social," I answered with a smile. "Vera and I are old friends. I stopped by to see if she was free for lunch, but I don't mean to interrupt a meeting."

"Why don't you join us? I'm taking Vera for a nice lunch, to fortify ourselves before a difficult afternoon."

"We're going to the wake for Kevin Conley," Vera said. "You know, the young man who was in the accident. We're sort of dreading it. It would be great to have you come to lunch with us."

"I'm not really dressed for going out anyplace nice—"

"You look fine," said Vera, who managed to

look cute in anything and whose indifference to clothes was notorious.

"You look terrific," said Elkan. I hoped it was true. I was just wearing pants and a short-sleeved shirt, but they were good ones, and the pants fit very well. I hoped my plain gold hoop earrings could pass for elegant simplicity. I'd deal with the makeup as soon as I could. I liked that admiring gleam in Elkan's eye.

I assumed we'd turn into the nearest pub, but Elkan hailed a cab and whisked us a few blocks west and north, to the gleaming towers of the World Financial Center and a hushed, wood-paneled, glass-fronted second-floor restaurant with a view of the Hudson River where it flowed into New York Harbor. Elkan was greeted by name, and we were ushered to a table with a perfect harbor view.

The menu promised dishes based on fresh Hudson Valley produce and game, and wines from local boutique wineries. Just as I was wondering if this was an upscale gimmick, a theme restaurant more sophisticated than Trader Vic's, lightly disguised by the clubby atmosphere and the use of "free range" in the menu, Elkan looked up and said, "It tastes as good as it reads. All that food-trendy stuff is true. I eat here a lot."

An interesting remark, I thought. He went on, "I'd recommend wine over a drink. The choices by the glass are unusual."

Vera shook her head. "I need to fortify myself with a Scotch. Maybe two."

"Kay?"

"Your turf," I said with a smile. "Surprise me with something great."

"Easily done."

A short conference with the waiter produced a terrific glass of Millbrook chardonnay. We would have fresh corn soup, a salad of local mixed greens and goat cheese, and warm salmon fillet with fresh tomato and coriander salsa. A perfect summer meal.

Talk over lunch was pleasant, superficial, and awkward, as we tried to a balance a three-way conversation and not drift into old friends' shorthand between Vera and me, business talk between Vera and Elkan, and getting-acquainted talk between Elkan and me. There were interludes of each. I observed that Vera and Elkan appeared to have a polite, not quite friendly working relationship. He seemed to know a lot more about her work than I assumed the owner of a large development company normally would.

In fact, Alan Elkan was a surprise to me in many ways. I didn't know I had any preconceptions about real estate magnates until I realized he didn't fit into any of them. He was not an elderly man with a tough attitude and a Brooklyn accent, who'd obviously fought his way up in a cutthroat business. He was not an oily and arrogant, self-congratulatory younger man with no education and flashy taste. He was not a courtly, old-line businessman whose family had been successfully building New York for generations.

He had some thoughtful and interesting points to make about architecture and the potential beauty of the riverfront. He told some witty and self-mocking stories about dealing with city agencies. And he never once mentioned money. If there were more like him in the building business, maybe I had underestimated my interest in covering real estate.

Lunch concluded, he excused himself, and I said to Vera, "How have you managed to stay businesslike? This guy's a charmer."

"Oh, he is that," she said dryly. "He charmed me into coming today instead of working on the site. I mean, we've lost a lot of time the last few days, and I barely knew the kid. I feel very sorry for the family and all, but I didn't really feel obligated to make this visit. Alan somehow convinced me that I was." She paused. "He'd charm me right into shutting down the dig, if he could. We may be slowing up his building, and I don't think he likes that much, though he's trying hard to be the culture-respecting entrepreneur. And that's part of the answer to your question. This is a business relationship, and I'm more interested in my career than Alan Elkan's brown eyes." She must have seen a question in mine, because she added, "Now, don't

look at me like that! I am. It took me way too long
to get serious, and now I'm making up for lost time.
Besides," she laughed and shrugged, "he's not my
type. Too lounge lizardy. You know I like the outdoor type."

"Yeah. Marlboro men."

"Well, if you must speak in stereotypes, in a
word, yes. Now you, on the other hand, do like
Alan's type."

"Not lounge lizards! And I don't think he's one
at all."

"Not really. But he is your type, and"—she
grinned—"he obviously thinks you're his."

"Don't be silly," I said dismissively, thinking it
might be true, and in another time and place, I
might be interested.

Alan returned, looking at his watch. "Vera, I arranged earlier for a car and driver in fifteen minutes.
He'll take us out to Queens and wait for us. Kay,
can we drop you somewhere?"

On an impulse, I said, "Can I come with you?"
Later, in the comfort of leather seats, powerful air-
conditioning, and heavy car smoothly driven
through traffic by a professional, I wondered why I
asked. Was I developing a morbid taste for funer-
als? Was I avoiding my office and my annoying
boss, or my lovely, empty apartment? Or was it
because, in my dreams, Kevin Conley's pale face
still sometimes looked up at me from the mud?

THREE

VERA, never a good midday drinker, proved her indifference to Alan's opinion by falling asleep in the comfortable car, but Alan and I chatted about the changing patchwork of neighborhoods we were passing through, trading experiences of the reporting and real estate life around the city.

Our destination turned out to be a neat, modest neighborhood of endless rows of two-story brick houses with garages built underneath. Once I would have thought, ''Narrow dull homes and narrow dull lives,'' but I've learned enough over time to recognize love and pride in those scrubbed front steps, the sculptured evergreen shrubs, the added-on porches, the bright rosebushes, the occasional religious shrines. A neighborhood where every man's small castle was hard-earned and valued. I thought I was already learning some things about Kevin Conley's family.

We drove down a neighborhood main street with a few bars, a coffee shop, a barber, small grocery stores, a dry cleaner, a newsstand/stationery/candy store. It looked as if nothing had changed in my lifetime, though I'd bet the groceries were now owned by Koreans, not Italians, and the candy store was probably Pakistani. I said as much to Alan, who laughed and said, "I know what you mean, but this is deepest Queens. Things don't change around here. Bet you a dollar?"

"Diamond Jim! Okay, you're on."

He asked the driver to stop at the next candy store, went in, and came out with sodas. Laughing, he handed me a dollar bill.

"You got me. It doesn't happen often when it comes to city life, but then, Queens isn't my turf. Don't think I'm not scheming about how to win it back."

A few more blocks and we were there, a dignified stone building rather like a small bank. Vera woke up suddenly and began to smooth her hair into place. I adjusted my slacks, fixed my earrings. Alan straightened his tie and his shirt cuffs.

I said to them, "Tell me what to expect today. I hardly know anything except his name and his age."

Vera yawned. "Ask Alan. His idea anyway."

Alan said, apologetically, "I have it all written down here. I can't know every man in every crew on my projects." He handed me a typed sheet of paper. Kevin Conley was twenty-four. Lived with his parents in Woodside. Graduated from Catholic high school. On the job two years.

"Not much to know, is there?"

"Nope. He was only a kid."

Alan looked out the window for a moment, then turned to the driver and told him to take a break and return in an hour. Taking a deep collective breath, we all went in together.

As we were signing the guest book, an older man, gray-haired, short, and powerfully built, came up to us with a grim expression and outstretched hand.

"Mr. Elkan."

"Jerry." They shook hands, and the other man said, "Good of you to come. Very good. It'll mean a lot. And Vera, too."

"Hello, Jerry. This is my friend Kay Engels. She was with me the night—"

"Now it's coming to me. I thought you looked familiar. Jerry Murtaugh. I let you in that night. Good of you to come today. Good of all of you."

"Jerry is site manager for the construction company. He supervises this whole phase, so I guess you'd say he was the boy's boss," Alan said.

"More than that, much more. I go all the way back with the Conleys, the whole family of them. I went to St. Augustine parochial school with Kev's uncle Brian, ushered at his parents' wedding, got Kevin his first job. So I'm here, helping out whatever way I can. Come on, I'll introduce you."

He led us to the couple receiving visitors at the other end of the room. I was shocked at how young they looked. They seemed only a few years older than I am. Was that possible? I did a quick calculation. Yes, it was, if they'd started young.

They would have been a handsome couple if there hadn't been so much pain in their faces. He was tall and big, with dark Irish good looks, in a black suit that was a little skimpy, as if he'd put on a bit of weight since the last funeral. She was small and blond, with heavily permed hair and a sweet face. They were flanked by two big, good-looking boys in dark suits, obviously Kevin's younger brothers.

Alan led the way, completely at ease in a room of curious strangers. When Jerry Murtaugh introduced him, Mr. Conley whispered something to his wife, and her eyes widened in surprise.

"Mr. Elkan...so good of you...," she stammered. "I never expected..." Her eyes filled.

"Now hush, Mary," her husband said gently, patting her shoulder. "Terry, get your mother a drink of water. Or would you like a cup of tea?" He shook Alan's hand. "Good of you to come. We appreciate it, especially the wife and boys." He nodded toward them.

"It's nothing," Alan said. "I wanted to express my sympathy in person, and ask if there's anything I can do. The firm sent a wreath, but is there anything else at all?"

"Oh, no, no, no," Mrs. Conley said. "Just talk

to me about my boy. Was he a good worker? Did you like him?''

"Certainly," Alan said promptly. "He was a pleasure to have on the crew. Jerry certainly agrees with that." He turned to the other man with a warning look.

Murtaugh nodded quickly and said, "Kevin was the best. You know I always thought so. He worked hard, learned fast, got along with everyone."

Alan added, "You raised a good boy."

She nodded fervently and said, "Thank you for telling me that. Thank you so much! He *was* a good boy…I was so proud…"

"Excuse me. I'm losing my manners here," Alan said gently, cutting short the sobs that seemed about to start. "I should have introduced Vera Contas, who's doing some archaeology at the site, and Kay Engels."

"I knew Kevin too, just a little," Vera said. Her voice was steady and calm, but I saw her hand shaking until she stopped it by wrapping her fingers tightly around the strap of her purse. "He was interested in what we were doing. He'd stop and ask questions, good questions too, and look at what we found. We talked. I was even encouraging him to volunteer sometime, so he could learn the techniques."

"Kevin always liked the old things," Mrs. Conley said. "These two lunks here, they'd die before going to a museum, but Kevin always liked the bones and the arrowheads and fossils. He told us a bit about you, Miss Contas, and what you were finding.''

''His interest was, well, it's a pleasure to see curiosity. He was—'' She seemed to be searching for words, and for the first time, her voice wavered. She held Mrs. Conley's hand for a moment. ''He was a good kid.''

I had been quietly observing everything, making myself as invisible as possible, but then Mr. Conley turned to me and said, ''You knew Kevin too?''

I didn't know what to say. All of a sudden I realized I didn't belong here, in this private place of grief. I wasn't even on a story. I had no excuse for my presence.

Alan stepped in smoothly. ''Ms. Engels was with Vera the night''—he finished very gently—''the night Kevin was found.''

Recovering myself at last, I said, ''I just wanted to meet you and say how very, very sorry I am.''

''My poor Kevin,'' his mother sobbed. ''You know, I never really wanted him in construction. He was smart, that boy. He could have done anything, but it was all he could ever see, to build like his dad and his uncles. I thought at least he'd be safe on the ground. No high steel, I said. No way. And now he's gone.'' Then she really did begin to cry, and her sons surrounded her.

Her husband moved away with us, saying apologetically, "He was so young, had his whole life ahead of him, work, wife, kids. The girls liked him, you know, but he wasn't for settling down yet. I always said—" He paused and turned away for a moment, taking a deep breath. "I always said, plenty of time for that."

Then he turned to Alan and said firmly, "I didn't want her to hear this, but I wanted to ask you. How come there was no watchman there? I just keep thinking, if only someone saw him fall. You know? If only help came sooner?"

"If you think like that," Alan said gently, "you'll go crazy. I talked to the ambulance team. They thought it must have happened instantly, but yes, you deserve an answer, and yes, there should have been a watchman. It's the construction company responsibility, of course, not ours, whether he worked for them or they contracted it out."

Murtaugh said, "We asked. He stepped away for a coffee, or maybe it was really a drink. He's not working for us anymore. You can go to the bank with that."

Conley nodded. "You lie awake, and you think, and you wonder. I don't even know why he went back there. Usually he went out with his buddies, or came home. If only he'd gone out for a few beers instead. He wasn't a big drinker, you know, like so many of the boys are. Never even had to worry about that." He shook his head, hard. "I haven't slept much." Then he shook all of our hands and said again, "Thank you for coming. I've got to get back to my wife now."

After he left, Alan said softly to Jerry Murtaugh, "You let me know if they need anything. I gather there's no family of his own, but was there a girl? Debts? Funeral expenses?"

"I'll find out. No special girl I know about, and I doubt there's debts. He wasn't a gambler, could afford his car, you know, just a regular kid, living at home, having fun on Saturday nights, but not in any trouble or nothing."

Alan nodded. "My lawyers say we have no liability, and they're right, but it was such a stupid, tragic accident, I'd like to do what I can." He took out a business card, wrote on it, and gave it to Murtaugh. "If anything does come up, give my secretary a call, okay?"

"Thanks, Mr. Elkan." He pocketed the card. "I will."

As we left the funeral home, Vera said, "Nice performance, Alan. You didn't even know Kevin."

I thought it was a nasty crack, but he only looked amused. "Of course not. He worked for the construction company. *They* work for me, and *they* subcontract some of the work. Crews come and go. But I wanted to comfort his mother, and I think I did that."

"And you talked to the ambulance crew? Right!"

"No," he said quietly, but with just a little edge in his voice, "but one of my assistants did. What difference does it make? It was the right thing to say."

Vera made a face at me behind his back.

We drove back to Manhattan in a somber mood, not saying much. Alan finally opened his attaché and said, "I hope you'll excuse me if I work for a little while. It's been a long day out of the office, and I have to go out tonight."

"Excuse you? I'd welcome the chance to get some work done," Vera said. "I have a journal in my purse demanding to be read."

I was content to be left alone to think about the afternoon. Over the years, I'd seen young people die, and interviewed grieving parents, and always managed to distance myself just enough. Somehow the Conleys had gotten to me, though their son's death was no more, and no less, tragic than any young person's accidental death. If it was an accident. Even a reporter has to admit that sometimes things are exactly what they seem, but something about this still bothered me. I kept thinking about what his father had said, not knowing why Kevin went back. There was no reason for him to be there. And there was no reason for the watchman not to be. And the boy who wasn't a heavy drinker, smelling like a drunk.

And then I went on thinking, remembering his father's other words. "If only he hadn't..." That was an emotion I'd heard expressed so many times before. If only. Yet this time, I couldn't seem to block the pain in their faces. I was tired, but when I closed my eyes, that was all I saw. Perhaps it was because I was there today just as a person, just as myself, not looking out from behind the duck blind of a reporter's role. I began to wonder how much the years behind the duck blind had made it possible for me to keep everything at a distance. All those years, I'd loved being the watcher, the questioner, the observer, the one with the story. Had I also loved being the outsider, the one not involved? I thought, sleepily, Howard is wrong. I do need a change. And even more, there is something I need to do when I get home. Tonight. No more putting it off.

The next thing I knew, the driver was crawling through cross-Manhattan rush-hour traffic and asking for my address, and I was hoping I hadn't been snoring in front of an attractive man I had just met. Opening my eyes just a slit, to check out the situation, I was relieved to see that he was absorbed in his work and wasn't even looking at me. With my arm shielding my face, I covertly wiped my eyes and around my mouth before I sat up, tranquilly smoothing my hair.

When we reached my building, Alan said with a smile and a warm, two-handed handshake, "It was a pleasure to meet you, Kay. I'm sure it will be something more fun next time, and I hope it will be soon."

Vera waved and said, "See you soon, babe. I'll call you later this week."

I had dinner, and puttered, and watched TV, and talked on the phone, and finally, late that evening, for the first time in my life, I wrote a letter to my mother.

FOUR

MY PARENTS were both dead before I finished college. We had so little in common, for so long, that when they died in their retirement home in Florida, within six months of each other, I shed some dutiful tears and got on with my life. It was hard for me to remember a time when their dull, complacent lives and limited aspirations had not felt like a suffocating blanket to me.

Almost twenty years later, back in my hometown for the first time since high school, I learned that they were not my parents at all. The person who told me meant to blackmail me with that knowledge, but I'm not sure now that he didn't free me instead.

I learned, gradually and through my own efforts, that my mother's cousin Sally, dimly remembered from my early childhood, was really my mother; and finally, that Sally was no cousin, but my adoptive mother's younger sister. There was no father listed on my birth certificate, and Sally's name was crossed out in my grandparents' family Bible. It wasn't hard to picture how the disgraced seventeen-year-old let her much older sister, childless after fifteen years of marriage, raise the baby. The perfect solution for everyone.

Part of me wanted to go to their Florida graves and scream at them until they came back and explained themselves and gave me some answers. And a few weeks ago another part of me, in the aftermath of my trip home, opened some of their boxes, in storage since their death, and found every crayoned, glue-smeared, wobbly-printed card I had ever made for either parent, every spelling certificate or writing award or science-fair blue ribbon I had ever won, every report card, and a whole folder of reports and projects. My senior-year term paper on freedom of the press was there, and so was my third-grade report, "The Camel, A Desert Animal." Every newspaper article that mentioned my name, and twelve years' worth of annual school pictures in a special frame. My graduation picture and my diploma, in matching silver frames. My christening dress, the blue satin costume from the one year I took ballet, and the tassel from my high-school graduation cap, with its little dangling gold numeral.

That person who looked over those boxes, and cried, had to admit they had loved me and had done their best, even if their best left me with enormous questions, enormous holes in my life. Well, the way to deal with questions is to dig for answers. When I was very small, my father used to call me Pop-corn, because, he said, I was always popping up with questions. And my talent for asking the right questions, and skill at getting the answers, had certainly served me well in my professional life. Now it was time to put it to work for me personally. If there were answers to be found, I was by God going to get them.

Sally was much younger than my mother, no more than middle-aged even now. She could easily still be alive. Most likely was, in fact. There was a Florida address for her in my mother's address book. It was nineteen years old, but it was a place to start.

I argued with myself about hiring a detective. I knew a good ex-cop who'd opened an agency, and some who'd worked on missing persons cases. I even have a friend who's a reporter on the *Miami Herald.* As efficient as asking for help would be, I balked. This was so personal. I couldn't miss the irony, of course: a woman who makes her living examining other people's lives flinches at having anyone look at hers. But I did flinch. And besides, all the numbers I needed were in my Rolodex at work. And something about today made me want to do it right now. I couldn't waste another day. Not even another hour.

It came to me as I typed, a short letter explaining that I'd been going through my parents' belongings, found the address, and wondered if there were any

family mementos she might like. I added that I had
dim but cherished memories of her from my early
childhood. I didn't want to tell her the truth and
take a chance on scaring her off.

When I was done, the letter read right, but it
didn't look right. I call around the world. I word-
process. I fax. I e-mail. I don't actually write letters,
but what I had to say looked all wrong on computer
paper. I rummaged around in my desk until I found
a very old box of personal stationery, off-white,
linen-weave, rose-bordered. I had no idea where it
came from, but it would do. I copied the letter
neatly, in ink, by hand, and went out at midnight
to drop it in a mailbox.

I TOSSED AND TURNED all night, and kept dreaming,
strangely, about a music box. I woke up with a
perfect picture in my mind of a chunky gold link
bracelet with a tiny music box attached like a
charm. It played "Waltz of the Flowers," and it
was covered with twinkly, colored jewels. It was
my most loved possession in second grade, and I
hadn't thought of it in two and a half decades. It
was a Christmas gift from Sally.

I BEGAN the next day with some interviews downtown, which put me conveniently near Vera's site
in the late afternoon. I talked my way in and finally

spotted her when she stood up suddenly and whistled to get her students' attention.

"Everyone come here for a minute," she shouted. I joined the group, and she waved when she saw me.

"We're finding something very interesting over here, and I wanted you to see it. Take a look." She was pointing at a greasy patch in the soil that I wouldn't even have noticed.

"This is a sign of fire," she explained. "That's no surprise. What other fire evidence have we found? Charles?"

A black kid with spectacular dreadlocks promptly answered, "Charred wood."

"And why hasn't it just rotted away?"

"Fire preserves."

"Good. What else? Jennifer?"

A girl with green-striped hair and rows of earrings in both ears replied, "Charred bones."

"Right. What we haven't known for sure is whether they were burned in cooking or a trash fire, or something more. Extensive signs of fire over here, inside the old walls, and with no hearth, tell us it may have been something else.

"Next indoor class, we'll look at the written records and see what we can learn. Okay. Back to work. And keep drinking water, boys and girls. It's a hot day."

She turned to me with a look of suppressed excitement.

"There's more, isn't there?"

She nodded. "I'll tell you in the office, but I'm just going to watch here for a minute, to see how they're doing."

A fair-skinned redhead slapped sunscreen on her bare, sunburned shoulders. An Asian girl bobbed in time to the music coming from her Walkman while she used graph paper and colored pencils to map a square of earth. She carefully adjusted the simple frame-and-string grid she had placed over the earth to define her subject. The dreadlocked boy gently sifted soil while his classmate, stripped to the waist and sweating, added soil to the sifter.

"They certainly don't look like budding young scholars, do they?"

"They are, though," Vera responded. "You think it's easy to crouch like that for hours in the sun? Would you like another short field lesson?"

"Oh, no," I said, laughing. "I remember." Vera made me try it once, when she thought I wasn't being sufficiently respectful of the work. That was the first time I'd visited her at a dig and asked why no one was digging.

Vera had shouted with laughter, and then said, "That's a Victorian idea! You've seen too many movies with hordes of native diggers in burnooses shoveling sand off the pyramids. Come on! In *this* century, we use bulldozers to scoop off the top layer. After that, it's trowel and sift, trowel and sift, and occasionally brush. Think, Kay! We're looking for things that are old and fragile, as elusive as markings in the soil. And everything has meaning. You can't barge in like a fool, hacking away and maybe destroying the very things you're looking for.''

I remembered her intensity, and I saw the same expression now, as she looked at her students wielding trowels with the delicacy and precision of surgeons with scalpels.

We turned away, toward the office, and she said softly, ''That inn I told you about, that I think was here?''

''The pirate's lair?''

She gave me an exasperated look. ''Cut the comedy. Yes, if you must call it that. It's known to have burned to the ground. Which is exactly what the evidence is starting to show for this site.''

''The plot thickens!''

''Cut it out, Kay. I'm serious about this.''

''I know. I'm sorry.''

''You can make it up to me by coming out for a bite to eat. It's almost quitting time.''

THE PHONE WAS RINGING when I walked into my apartment later that night. It was Tony. We had been playing telephone tag for several days, and hearing his voice live at last made me smile all over. I was dismayed by how happy I was, and tried to cool down before answering his "How have you been?"

I could picture him in his office, door closed, feet up, tie loose, white shirtsleeves rolled partway up tanned arms, a special look, half-laughing, in his dark eyes while we talked. I have to admit I liked what I saw in my mind's eye.

Or maybe he'd knocked off early on this beautiful summer day and was already at his cottage on Lake Ontario. He'd be barefoot, in old cut-off jeans, lounging on the porch swing facing the sparkling lake. Probably there was the smell of hamburgers and fresh corn cooking on the grill, and the static I heard was coming from a portable phone used outdoors.

"Where are you? At the lake? I'm trying to picture you talking to me."

"You'd never succeed. I'm on a plane, about thirty thousand feet in the air."

"Tell me you're on the way to New York!"

"No. I wish. Kay, I'm on my way to Sydney."

"Sydney? As in Australia?"

"That's right. Strictly speaking, I'm on my way to Detroit, to get my kids first."

"But why? Why Sydney?" Why didn't you tell me you had a vacation planned? I thought.

"It's business."

I was confused. "Many Australian businesses in upstate New York?"

"No, of course not. An old, good client from my Wall Street days is doing a deal there, a follow-up of something I worked on, and he's convinced he needs me to help see it through."

"You're bringing your daughters?"

"It's my time to have them with me, and I told him I couldn't back out of it, and wouldn't if I could, so he said to bring them along. His people will arrange sight-seeing and child care and stuff for them. It's crazy, but we'll be in Sydney soon, with a stopover in Hawaii. It seems to take several days just to get there."

"It does, and it's always tomorrow or yesterday or something when you do. How long will you be there?"

"That's the worst part. I don't know, but several weeks at least. I miss you already; I don't know when we'll get together next."

I just managed to say lightly, "We'll just have to wait and see, then, won't we?"

"It won't be a minute longer than it has to be, I promise. Ah, they just made the landing announcement. Got to go. What do you want from Australia?"

I didn't say, "You." I didn't say anything.

"I'll call when I can," he said, "and I'll send

you my address. Write to me!'' The phone crackled, and he was gone.

''You won't like it,'' I said to the dead receiver. ''I've been there. It's very beautiful and very dull. And it's winter now.'' I knew I wouldn't hear from him for days. He'd be caught up in the rush to get his daughters ready, and dealing with his ex-wife. And once he was there, we'd never be able to connect on the phone. We'd never be awake at the same time.

FIVE

MY LIFE WENT ON. My letter to my mother came back stamped Addressee Unknown. I expected that. I did. Certainly I did. I didn't know, until the letter was in my hand, how much I had been hoping, against all sense and my own cynicism, for better results. It was time to call my friend at the *Miami Herald*.

After we'd spent time catching up, I asked my question. "What's the easiest way to trace someone through Florida public records when you only have a nineteen-year-old address?"

"Why, Kay," she said, suddenly wary, "what's all this about? Are you poaching a story in my backyard?"

"Actually, it's personal," I said, taking a deep breath. "I'm looking for a long-lost relative."

She responded with a hoot of laughter. "I've heard that one before! I expected a better story from you."

"Come on, Marsha. I feel dumb enough saying it, but it's the truth. I *would* make up a better story, if I was making one up."

"Whole truth? This relative isn't a Ten Most

Wanted or anything? You're not going to write a story my editor will give me hell for missing?''

"Would I do that to you?"

"Yes," she answered promptly. "And I would do it to you, but I don't think we'd ask each other's help to do it. That would be *too* low. I think. Is this relative story the truth?"

"Yes, it is."

"I can do it for you. It's easier to do than to explain. Just tell me what you've got." I did. "Okay. It sure isn't much, but I'll see what I can do. It might take me some time to get to it. You owe me a dinner next time I'm up north."

"Of course. There's this great new place, very in, called"—I chuckled—"Key West. All palm trees and oranges and seafood. Lots of coconut on everything."

"Very funny. I'll be expecting a New York strip steak, about sixteen ounces, and a large slab of cheesecake, honey. Talk to you soon."

Marsha is smart and resourceful. I had to trust her and be patient, or fly to Miami myself. And I couldn't ask for more time off just now.

In the meantime, my life in the city began to catch me up again. In late summer New York offers its stay-at-home citizens compensation for the hot and humid weather. There's an eerie, unreal, but not unpleasant impression of emptiness. It's easier to get around. Parking becomes possible everywhere, restaurant reservations are no problem, tickets to a hit show become a possibility.

I cooled off one day at lunchtime watching the penguins in the Central Park zoo. I heard old-time rock and roll at a crowded club in Greenwich Village with uncomfortable seats and lousy food, and a famous interpreter of Cole Porter at a Fifth Avenue hotel where the silver is silver and some of the crowd wore black tie. I went to different exotic restaurants every night.

In all that time, in idle moments, I would find myself imagining a woman with red hair and a deep laugh, and I'd be straining to bring her face into focus. One late night I had an inexplicable impulse to rearrange the shelf that held my oldest books. Or perhaps the impulse was not so inexplicable after all, because I found a copy of the Arabian Nights that I had all but forgotten. It had beautiful, old-fashioned color plates, richly colored, detailed and exotic. I remembered studying the pictures, enthralled, before I could even read, and I found again the inscription, "Happy birthday, dear Kay. Love, Sally." I almost saw her face that night in a dream. I know I heard her voice.

ONE OF THE FRIENDS I saw for dinner was Vera. We chatted about trivialities, but her usual humor wasn't in place, and she was avoiding talking about work for the first time in years. Even when she was unhappy at work, which was often, she always had a lot to say about it, some of it quite humorous. Finally I asked her about it straight out.

She sighed. "I didn't want to say anything, because it's all so nebulous."

"Not finding what you expected?"

"No, that's just it. I am, and I think there's a lot more."

"Then?"

"There's more vandalism than I ever had here. People have been in the shed at night. Stuff is rearranged, broken, missing." She anticipated my next question. "No, nothing valuable. I mean, this is New York, not some isolated forest. Anything important goes home with me or gets sent up to my office at the college. Lately I've started hiding what I find and smuggling it out so no one knows I found anything."

"It's that bad?"

"That's just it. I don't *know* if it's that bad or if I'm seeing monsters in the closet. It means so much to me, if this is what I think it is, maybe I'm overreacting."

"Doesn't sound like you."

"Thank you for that. It's nice to hear someone else say it. The most ridiculous part of it," she added, "is that most of what we find is completely valueless in the real world sense. It's not King Tut's tomb, for crying out loud! It's not even copper

pipes that junkies could steal out of an abandoned
building. It's all historical value, what it means. To
anyone but a historian or archaeologist, it's just
junk. I don't understand it.''

"Now, wait. Haven't I seen stories about illegal
sales of antiquities? Stealing from archaeological
sites?''

"Yes, yes,'' she agreed impatiently, "it goes on
and it's serious, but nothing I've found is old
enough or rare enough to mean anything in that
market. It's not pre-Columbian art or Roman coins.
You saw. It's pottery, glass, yes, a few coins, nothing big. There's no treasure. Not even something
dramatic, like bones. It's all extremely pointless, as
far as I can see, but extremely annoying.''

I tried to picture the site. "It's a very big lot,
isn't it? And there's construction on part of it already?''

She nodded.

"What I'm wondering is, what is happening at
the rest of the site? Any problems there, or does it
seem directed at you?''

"Not a one, or at least none they're telling me
about. And another thing—the construction company isn't concerned about this at all as a security
problem. I'm not even sure they believe me. That's
why I appreciated you saying I don't overreact.
They seem to think I'm imagining it. You know, a
ditzy dame misplacing her finds.''

"Not really! That's what they think?"

"They haven't come right out and said it, but that's kind of the feeling I get. I hate being patronized like that. They wouldn't do it to a man, or even a big woman with a deep voice." She saw my exasperated look and said, "Okay, okay, that's not the point here."

"Right. The point is what is actually happening and why. You have a crew working with you, don't you? What do they think?"

"Nothing. They're all students, too inexperienced to notice or to know that something is different here."

I remembered something. "The night we found that young man's body, wasn't there some talk about a watchman who should have been there? Shouldn't there be some kind of security?"

"You're right about that night, and yes, there should be. There's too much building material and machinery around to leave it open to anyone. What I heard about that night is that he was off having coffee, or a drink most likely, and he was fired. The new watchman never seems to see or hear a thing."

We left the restaurant and were walking west toward the river, hoping to catch a breeze, when Vera turned to me suddenly and said, "Kay, come with me right now."

"What?"

"Come downtown to the site. We can surprise

that watchman, maybe catching him goofing off, and you can be my witness. Then maybe I can get a response from Carson Construction. I can throw it in their faces.''

"Vera, you do know you are crazy."

"Yes, but I'm fed up. I don't think it's dangerous, and I am authorized to be there. Listen, if nothing else, maybe your objective eye on the scene will help me see things more sensibly." She knew my weak spot, and moved in on it. "Come on! Admit it! You're curious, aren't you? Anyway, I'm going with or without you.''

Yes, I was curious. And I wasn't anxious to go back to my lonely apartment either. And I was bored with the stories I was getting assigned. And I knew Vera would go alone. That was definitely a dumb idea, but I'd seen that hell-bent look on her face before. And those are the reasons I found myself driving downtown to the dark streets of the financial district at 11:00 p.m.

It was quiet, but there was a little street traffic and the occasional passerby on foot. In every stock brokerage and law office ambitious, overworked young professionals were still crunching numbers or researching statutes. There were cleaning crews at work in every office tower. I wondered when the district truly shut down. I didn't know. I'd never been there late enough.

Vera wasn't looking around. She was wound up,

walking purposefully to the locked gate and using her own key to let us in. The streets were lit well enough by streetlights, but it was much darker inside the construction fence. Once again I found myself cautiously following Vera onto the site. She pointed to the first shed inside the gate and whispered, "There. That's where the watchman should be, unless he's walking around, and I sure don't see a bright flashlight waving around out there." Her gesture encompassed the whole building site.

She rapped sharply on the door and gently pushed it open. "Just as I thought. No one here. That slug. Let's take a walk and see if we can find him."

We circled the site slowly, never seeing a light or a sign of him in any of the trailers. We ended at Vera's own shed.

"Vera—" I held her back.

"It's all *right,* Kay. Look. Padlock's locked. No lights inside. No windows open. It's my own office, after all. I certainly have a right to go into it."

She unlocked the door, reached up to flip the light on, and gasped. I was right behind her and saw what she saw.

The makeshift office had been wrecked. Furniture was toppled over, drawers dumped, papers thrown around. The few artifacts Vera kept there were smashed into fragments of pottery and glass on the floor. The cheap laminate desk had been gashed repeatedly. The locks on the file cabinet were broken.

Vera slumped down on the steps. The fiery Vera of a few minutes ago was gone. "See," she whispered. "I wasn't imagining it. I wasn't."

SIX

I KNELT BESIDE HER, took her hands, and said, "What do you want me to do?"

She shook her head slowly. "I need to think—this is so stupid—they broke locks that weren't locked—destroyed things that weren't important—" She shook her head again, sharply, as if to clear it. "I have to get a grip. They ripped out my phone, but there's one in the main office trailer. We'll call the Carson office, and the security company."

"Police?"

"Let the Carson guys do it. It's too weird for me to do it a second time." She gave me a shaky but determined smile and said, "I'll be all right. Let's go."

We walked slowly back toward the gate. The office trailer, where the watchman should have been, was still lit up and still empty, and the front gate was still locked, just as we had left it, with my car parked right in front of it.

I was just going into the trailer when I heard a crash, like glass breaking, and just caught, out of the corner of my eye, flashing lights and a confusion of movement. I walked right up to the gate to look at my car, and my stomach turned over. The windshield was smashed. In the light from the streetlamp I could see the jagged edges clinging to the frame, and on the ground, a layer of pebble-size fragments of bluish glass glittering like pale jewels.

When I went back into the trailer, Vera never noticed there was something wrong with me. Her fear had transformed itself into fury, and she was already yelling at someone on the phone when I went into the trailer.

I picked her keys up off the table and went back out to unlock the gate and take a look at my violated car.

It was even worse than I thought. The headlights were smashed, and two tires were flat. I swallowed hard. The ignition lock hadn't been touched, which made this look more like deliberate vandalism than attempted car theft. The random violence of angry urban youths? Maybe, but I wondered then why it stopped where it did. The upholstery wasn't harmed. There was no fire. Nothing saleable, such as tires or battery, had been stolen. My car was an old one, a battered Volvo bought in Europe when I lived there. It was beat-up and ugly but 100 percent reliable, and I was very fond of it. I felt as if I had been attacked, and I shuddered. What was really going on here?

I turned back to the trailer, angry about my car, angry about what had been done to Vera's office,

angry at Vera for getting me into this. I couldn't
tell her so until she finished her argument and
slammed the phone down.

"He'll be here," she said with grim satisfaction.
"He said to wait right here. Now I'll get some action from these jerks."

Vera finally looked at my face.

"Kay? What's up?" I waved a hand toward the
outside, toward my car. She went out to see, looking puzzled, and came back looking sick.

"Vera, what is really going on here? I think you
owe me some details."

"What do you mean?"

"'What do you mean?'" I mimicked. "My car's
just been destroyed, your office is destroyed—"

"You don't think it's coincidence?"

"No, and neither do you. This is looking very
ugly."

"Okay, okay." She paused. "I know it is. I do
know, but I don't know what it's about, not for
sure. Kay, don't look at me like that! I'm not being
evasive on purpose."

"Then tell me what you *think* it's all about, right
now, before we have to deal with construction people, tow trucks, and who knows what else."

She took a deep breath. "I think someone is trying to stop this dig. I was beginning to think so

before, and now, well, doesn't it look like someone wants to scare me away?''

It certainly did. And if not, then something else here was very wrong, and I was becoming extremly interested in finding out what it was. My editor had said there wasn't a story; tonight's events were saying otherwise. Shouting otherwise. I just didn't know yet exactly what the story was. I didn't, but I would.

"Maybe they thought my car was yours."

Vera nodded. "There's no reason at all for—whoever—to attack you."

"Do you think it's Alan Elkan? It's his building. He must be anxious not to have delays."

She shook her head slowly. "I don't think so. He's been pretty helpful all along. Comes by to see how we're doing and asks intelligent questions."

I wasn't convinced, but I kept my opinion to myself. "Then who?"

"I keep thinking it's Carson, you know, the construction company, but it's not anything they've done. It's more what they haven't done, the way they've ignored my complaints—I know they want me to find nothing important, finish here, close up, and get out of their way."

I didn't think they could ignore my smashed car, sitting like a large island in a lagoon of turquoise broken glass. They couldn't ignore her trashed office. Whatever was or was not going on earlier, to-night was real. Too real.

"Kay," Vera said, "do me a favor?"

I gave her an unfriendly look.

"No, no, it's easy. Just listen and watch when Murtaugh shows up. He's the manager from Carson. See if you see what I see, and anything I miss, too." She rubbed her eyes with a weary gesture. "I know I'm too involved. I need someone else's eyes to pick up what's happening." She smiled, wearily. "You're the best observer I know."

"I'll do it. I have to wait for the tow truck anyway, and I'd like a word with this Murtaugh myself."

"You've met him, you know. Kevin Delaney's funeral."

"Older man? Introduced us?"

"That's him."

"He seemed pleasant enough."

"Yes, very. That's why I'm glad you're here. Look behind that. Pretend he's a politician."

I had to smile. However irritated I was at Vera, it's hard to stay angry at someone who knows me so well.

When Murtaugh arrived, he certainly seemed shocked by the sight of Vera's office.

"Vera, I don't know what to say. Our security service has a lot of explaining to do here. We contracted for an all-night guard, but you know it's hard to get reliable people for this line of work. I'll certainly be raising hell with them first thing tomorrow morning."

"I think you waited too long," Vera snapped. Her temper was up again. "I've been complaining about security for days. Why did you have to wait for something like this? And let me show you my friend's car."

She guided him out of her office and over to the gate. His first reaction was, "It's not on our property. It could be any random street vandalism. Happens all the time."

"Oh, give me a break! Does this look like the kind of neighborhood where wild kids come to party and then get their kicks destroying property? Lots of clubs around here? Seen many crack addicts on Wall Street lately, even at night?"

"All right, all right, it might be the same person, but, miss," he turned to me, "sorry as I am that it happened, I don't see that we have any responsibility here."

"You have some responsibility to me," Vera insisted.

"Yes, I believe we do. Subject to a talk with our lawyers, and not holding me to anything now, security is our responsibility. Lawyers already told me we have to report it to the police. I have to tell you, though, I don't know how seriously they'll take it."

"What do you mean by that?"

He shrugged. "Don't get me wrong. I'm not saying it's not for real, and personally, I think it stinks. I wouldn't want this to happen to either of you ladies, or anything like this on any project of mine anytime. It's just that no one was hurt, and nothing valuable stolen. They have more pressing business. They'll come, they'll make a report, but I'm betting that's it. One more act of senseless vandalism added to all the others. You know?"

"Two," I said. "Two acts of vandalism."

"Okay, okay, two. Some wino or crackhead—" He paused, then said very carefully, very calmly, "Has it occurred to you that maybe this is just more trouble than it's worth? And it's even getting a little dangerous?"

"Go on."

"You say there's been little things before. Now this. And poor Kevin's death, too, an accident of course, but if it was me, I'd be feeling a little spooky."

"I deal with grave sites and bones, Mr. Murtaugh. It's my job." Vera said. "I don't spook easily."

I noticed that she called him Mister, and thought I remembered they had been on a first-name basis before.

He shrugged again. "Maybe you're right about this not being a dangerous neighborhood, but it looks to me like it's getting too dangerous for you anyway. How important can a few dug-up old things be, compared to your safety and all? Kevin's death was real hard to take. I just don't want to see anyone else hurt here." He turned back to the watchman's shed. "Let's call the cops and get that over with." He smiled. "And would you like to hear me chew out our security company? I'll call their night line right now."

He left a blistering message, demanding an immediate response from a company officer and an immediate replacement for the missing watchman, and then called the police. We settled down to wait, expecting it to be a long night, but the phone rang almost immediately.

"Murtaugh here." He listened, then said, "I don't know where your man is, and I don't care. Sleeping it off somewhere, probably—You bet. Two, and right away—Yeah, I'll hold—Yes, and damn quick too. We'll have a meeting in the morning, my office."

He turned to us. "They're pulling two guards from another location nearby, and I'm gonna speed things up by going to get them. You feel okay about being here alone? If you keep the gates locked? Or, I don't know, maybe you want to come with me?"

"What I really want," Vera said, "is to start cleaning up my office, instead of just sitting around."

"Can't do it yet. Cops said touch nothing."

"I know, I know. But I could just look. Maybe make a list of what's missing and so on."

I said, "Someone's got to wait for the police anyway, to let them in. And I have calls to start making. I'll stay right here in the office, where I can watch the gate."

"I'll be back in a flash. Not a chance they'll get here before I get back. Let me out, would you? And lock everything behind me!"

He was gone, and Vera started back toward her office. I knew how she felt. I wanted to be doing something too, namely assessing the damage to my car and calling a tow truck. Arranging a car rental. Calling my insurance agent. I knew I should restrain myself until after the police came. The watchman had a tiny TV in the trailer. I turned it on and found myself watching *All in the Family* at 1:00 a.m. The night was very quiet now. The faint sound of an occasional car was all I heard. I wasn't nervous being alone. Vera and I were sure the vandal was gone, and I knew there would be a small crowd of public and private uniforms any minute. I may even have nodded off, because when Vera screamed, it seemed to come from a long way away.

I tore out of the trailer and ran toward the light of her office. I didn't hear another scream.

She stumbled out to meet me, and I caught her.

"Are you all right? Are you?"

"Yes, yes," she gasped. "Oh, Kay, I'm all right, but someone just shot out my window. It just missed me, there's glass everywhere, I was scared to death." She saw my face then, and smiled a shaky smile. "I'm sorry. I scared you to death too, didn't I?"

"You sure did. Are you really all right?"

"Yes." She nodded and shivered. "One more thing to tell the police." Murtaugh arrived with the security guards. He gave them their orders, and they went to patrol the site while we told him of the latest event.

He looked shocked and said, "I truthfully don't know what to think, and I've never seen something like this in thirty years in construction. You sure it was a bullet?"

"I don't know anything else it could have been."

"We'll leave it to the cops to figure it out. I just can't believe it. Now, trying to steal building materials, sure. I even know about someone who was trying to steal a truck, couple parts at a time. That one wasn't too bright! Graffiti, sure. Bums hanging out in site trailers. But this night is nuts." He shook his head and said again, "The cops'll have to figure out if it was a shooting." Then he turned to me. "What are you going to do about your car?"

"Get it towed, I guess. And then deal with the

insurance company. I could have done without the aggravation."

"Yeah, I know. Nothing worse. You have a good body shop? I could send you to a guy I know, very good work, and he can be very helpful about how he writes up a bill, if you know what I mean. I could call him right now."

"Now? In the middle of the night?"

"Not a problem. He'd be happy to oblige. He'll send a truck."

The officers came at last, two men, one young, one older, both white, one with a mustache. They looked over the car and gave me some forms. They looked at Vera's office, listened to her story about the gunshot, examined the shattered office window, and looked all over for a bullet. They did find it at last, where it had rolled under some of the other debris. They were polite and thorough and unimpressed. I took their names and badge numbers while they took our reports.

They left promising to get in touch if anything turned up. When I pressed them to tell us if they thought anything would, the older cop said, "Miss, we'll do our job, but let me be up front with you, okay? This has been tough on all of you, and I don't want to give you false hopes, and I would deny even in court I ever said it, and my partner would back me, but, bottom line: Don't count on it. A gun was used, and of course we take that seriously, but no one hurt? Nothing valuable taken? No real evidence left behind? How much do you think we can really do?''

Murtaugh called a tow truck, which appeared with astonishing speed. I wondered how he could have arranged that. My car was taken to the body shop he recommended, to be safely locked up overnight. The driver gave me a card and said, ''Call late tomorrow.''

We persuaded Vera to leave her office alone until morning, and we went home in the cabs Murtaugh found for us. I collapsed instantly into restless sleep and dreamed I was talking to an attractive man whose face I couldn't quite see. We were together somewhere vague, and I was leaning against him, telling all about the events of the night. He didn't say anything that I could remember, but I was infinitely comforted.

I woke up halfway, in my restless sleep, just enough to know I was dreaming. I was too sleepy to figure out whether the pang I felt was because it was only a dream, or because I was dreaming about leaning on someone.

SEVEN

BEFORE I WAS FULLY AWAKE the next morning, Vera was at my door. As she walked in, she was saying, "I called your office. They said you were still home. We have to talk."

"Well, hello to you too, and how are *you* after the events of last night?"

"Cut it out, Kay. I'm just too distracted for the amenities." She paced up and down my small living room. "Listen. I really need your help. Last night, the cops, I know they took it seriously in a way. They know something happened, and they'll do what they can, but how important is it to them, really? Not very, I bet." I more than agreed with her. Her small faith in them was still bigger than mine. I was sure it was of no importance, and nothing would be done, but I kept that thought to myself and let her continue.

"No matter what, it can't be as important to them as it is to me. I'm running out of time." She stopped abruptly, as if catching her breath or gathering her arguments.

"So?"

"Kay, it's like this. I only have two more weeks. That was the deal Alan made with the agencies. I get just so long to investigate the site. If nothing important turns up, that's it. I stop, they close up and start building."

"So?"

"I know there's something important there. I know it! I told you what I expect to find." She took a deep breath. "Kay, if I'm prevented from working this week, those bulldozers will be in there in a few days no matter what I say. This is my chance, my real chance. After all these years always struggling to be taken seriously, struggling for grants and funding, still living like a grad student at my age. Listen. If this is as big as I think, my name will be made. Jobs will come to me, instead of me chasing them. It's time, dammit. I've earned it."

"Yes, you have," I said. Oh yes, I knew how she felt. We had spent some long years fighting our way in and up, and had some of the same scars to show for it. "All right, Vera, you have my attention, and you have my sympathy, but if you don't tell me what you really want, in *exactly* ten seconds, you go out the door."

She gave me an exasperated look and said again, "Are you a little slow from lack of sleep? Isn't it obvious? I want you to write a story about this. If people sort of know what's going on, and what I might be finding, it will scare away whoever is harassing me."

"I can't do it just like that! I'm planning to suggest it. *Something* sure as hell is going on, but it's only a story when an editor says so. It might be too local. I don't work for a daily paper anymore! Don't you ever read the magazine?''

She looked abashed. ''Not often. I wasn't thinking. But you could *push*, couldn't you?'' Her expression brightened. ''And you could try to figure out what's going on.''

''Vera,'' I said carefully. I was speaking in precisely the voice I would use with an armed lunatic. I didn't quite say, ''I know you don't want to hurt anyone, so why don't you just put the gun down?'' I said, ''It's been a rough week, all in all, but you know I can't play cop.''

''That isn't what I meant! I haven't completely lost my mind. But maybe the real cops won't do anything. Or maybe it will take too long. Haven't you been listening? I need to get on with my work, right now, this week, today! I can't wait for the mills of official justice.

''You could ask questions for me. You do it for a living; do it for me. Elkan likes you. Talk to him, find out what he thinks, see if he knows anything. You get answers from people.''

''I'm not some kind of double agent. You should be hiring a professional investigator or detective. I could find you someone—''

''I don't have the money. I have just about two weeks' worth of expenses in my checking account." She looked at me defiantly, then suddenly rested her head on her hand in a gesture of infinite weariness and said in a small voice, almost a whisper, "I'm desperate, Kay. Please."

And maybe that is why I did finally say yes. I have long years of practice resisting when Vera pushes, and long years of practice pushing back. She'd never begged me before. And maybe my wrecked car had something to do with it too.

Later that morning I went straight to my editor. I pushed. "It's all kind of crazy, Howard. The vandalism is real enough, and so was that bullet, and none of it makes sense. I don't know what it's all about, yet, but it's *something*. I feel it—especially after seeing my car!"

"Would you like to go back to some safe overseas assignment? Sarajevo, maybe?"

I gave him a dirty look, and he said, "All right, all right, I'll quit joking. It's not a story for a national magazine, not yet, but *if* your friend finds something really big, or *if* a major crime occurs, then yes, we're interested. Sure." Before I could even ask the next question, he answered it. "Yes, yes, treat it as an idea in development. Start collecting background. And let me know if anything else happens." He waved me out, then added, "And Kay, sorry about your car." Sometimes he gets me off guard with a human comment like that.

I called Vera to let her know where things stood

and promised I'd be in touch. Then I went downstairs to the library to put in a research request for everything they could find on Alan Elkan and his business, and for good measure, I added Carson Construction. My friend Nancy was on the desk when I walked in.

"When do you need it, Kay? Is it on deadline?"

I hesitated, wondering if I should lie about that to get it more quickly. Nancy laughed.

"I know that look! It isn't, or you'd say so instantly and demand it yesterday!"

"You're right," I admitted. "It's background, so I can take it whenever you can do it."

"Maybe tomorrow. At least a first pass, the easy-to-find stuff. Will that be okay?"

"That's fine. Thanks."

I talked to the body shop owner, who sounded grim but said to call back tomorrow. I made a few calls to follow up on the police, but didn't learn anything except whom to call next. I decided a personal visit to the law was the next order of business. Just before I was ready to leave, Alan Elkan called.

"Kay, are you all right? I just heard about last night from my project manager. Gave him hell, too, for not calling me on the spot."

I was startled by his intensity. "What did he tell you? I'm all right, just upset and angry. My car is a mess, and it's probably too old to be repaired."

"What kind is it?"

"Volvo. Very old. I bought it in Europe years ago."

"I know a great body shop, very reliable, and I can guarantee it. I own the building they're in. Just tell me where it is now, and I'll take care of it."

"No really, Alan, that's not necessary. I do appreciate it, but your Mr. Murtaugh got a tow truck last night and sent it to a place he swore was good. Premier, out on Coney Island Avenue."

"Great. That's my place. Now, you'll call me if I can help with anything? Promise?"

"Yes, yes, I promise."

"Good. Now, can you tell me what really happened? Or better yet, how about over dinner tonight? I'd really like to do something to make it up to you. And I bet you could use some fun, after last night."

I hesitated, and he added, "That is, if you're free on short notice. You name the kind of place, whatever you're in the mood for: cozy and restful, loud and distracting, glamour night on the town."

Suddenly, it did sound as if it was just what I needed. I wasn't sure if his suggestion was guilt or fear of negative publicity or a date, but I didn't care. It was only dinner. I didn't really want another man in my life, but Tony wasn't there, wasn't even reachable, was barely in my life, and it was, after all, only dinner. Someone taking me out for fun and distraction suddenly sounded very, very appealing.

I felt like a child looking for comfort in a lollipop. Any flavor would do.

"Yes, I can be free," I said. "Maybe someplace quiet but fun? Is that possible?"

"Absolutely. Seven-thirty okay?"

At the very least, it would prevent me from sitting home alone, obsessing about the battles with my car insurance company that loomed ahead. At most, I would have a great dinner, and maybe learn a little more from Alan Elkan about what was happening at Vera's dig.

I headed downtown to talk to the police officers who'd be looking into last night's incident. I hadn't done city news reporting in years, but I didn't think I'd forgotten how. I had a few names, and I was just going to start by asking questions, and keep asking them until I found someone who was friendly enough, bored enough, or trusting enough to answer them. Or until I annoyed someone so much he'd answer them just to make me go away.

That morning the subway system let me down. Due to mechanical problems somewhere down the line, my train was rerouted, and I found myself getting out near Vera's work site. Oh well, I wanted to talk to people who worked in the nearby building, to see if anyone had seen or heard anything, but I'd planned to do it in the evening, when I thought the chances were greater that the same nighttime staff would be there. On the other hand, there I was, so maybe I could ask a few questions now, get some names, save some time later.

At the first building a friendly and flirtatious young security guard confirmed that no one there now was there last night, but offered the names of the men who had been, and even checked to see which ones were scheduled to be on tonight. He pointed out with a wink that he'd be getting off when they came on, and he was a lot cuter than any of them. I laughed, agreed, and said thanks, but I had to work tonight.

At the second building I had the bad luck to run into a supervisor, who said I would not be permitted to ask his men questions unless I were the police, and that under no circumstances would he give out names. He then politely, but implacably, escorted me off the premises.

The third building was the one where Vera went to wash up the first night I visited her. The first guard I approached said, "Yeah, you're in luck. One of the night guys is right over there, talking to his buddy. He came by to pick up something."

He was a round-faced older man, pink-cheeked and bald, with a gray fringe of hair.

"Mr. Earl?" I said, after a quick glance at his badge.

"How can I help you, miss?"

"We met last week," I said with my best disarming smile. "It was quite late. I waited while my friend Vera used the rest room to wash up."

He broke into a grin. "Vera! What a great girl! Brings me coffee, stops and chats. I'm busy around six, when folks start having to sign out, but it gets real dull later. I enjoy seeing her. Oh, sure I remember you." He lowered his voice. "I really shouldn't be letting her—you understand—but I figure, where's the harm? There isn't any trouble about that, is there?"

"No, not at all, and she's grateful to have a place to wash. But I wondered if we could talk a minute?"

"Sure." He strolled down the lobby with me, away from the crowds. "Hey, how is Vera? She hasn't been around lately at all."

"She's had a lot on her mind, and then last night, well, her office was vandalized."

"Not again!"

"What? It's happened before?"

"Not to her, at least not that I've heard, but there have been others. Poor kid! Did she see anything? She wasn't hurt, was she?"

"No to both, but she's extremely upset and frightened. That's why she wanted me to ask around for her. She's just too upset to deal with it now." I was cheerfully slandering Vera without a single pang of conscience. She was more angry than upset, and the fragile picture I was drawing was not the Vera I knew and loved. However, this older man's attitude seemed rather protective, and I would say whatever encouraged him to talk. If making her look pathetically vulnerable was what it took, so be it.

"Poor kid," he said again. "Who would do that to her?"

"We'd like to find out, and that's really why I came to talk to you. I was wondering if you were here that night, and if you saw or heard anything."

"Last night? Yes, I was here, but I can't tell you a thing. I sit inside, right over there, not even too near the door, so something would have to be happening right outside, just about in front, for me to even notice."

"I see. But what did you mean when you said, 'not again'?"

"Oh, that." He looked uncomfortable. "I shouldn't be talking about it."

I took out my trump card. "Mr. Earl, someone shot at Vera."

"Jesus H. Christ. What's this world coming to? You did say she's all right?"

"Yes, she's just very shaky. But anything you know could be helpful. I'll be sure to pass it on to her."

"Yeah, well, maybe I do know something. See, the building owners don't want it to get around, they don't want these high-class, high-*price* tenants to get nervous, but I happen to know there's been a whole bunch of vandalism around here lately."

"What kind? I mean, what's happened? And when?"

"Real late at night, from what I hear from some of the other guys. It hasn't happened here. No one's seen anyone, but there's spray-painting, broken glass, that kind of stuff. So far the building's been able to clean it up in the early morning, so no one knows."

"Police?"

"I heard they're raising hell at the precinct. And of course police headquarters are only a little way from here too. This type of thing isn't supposed to happen on Wall Street, you know." He said it with a sarcastic grin.

"Have you heard about anything violent happening?"

"No, but you know, the incidents do seem to be getting worse, so maybe whoever it is is working up to something."

"Could be." What happened last night looked more personal than what he described, but it was interesting, and I knew just how to follow it up.

"Excuse me, miss, but I've got to get back to my errands."

"Yes, of course, and I appreciate your help. If you should happen to remember anything at all— you know, something might just pop up in your memory—could you call me?'' I gave him one of my plain cards, with my home phone.

"So long, Miss Engels. Nice to see you again. Give Vera my best and tell her to come around when she's up to it.''

"I'll definitely do that.''

I walked over to the police station. I'd just started trying to locate the officers who'd been there the other night when I heard a familiar voice behind me.

"Is that Kay Engels poking her nose into police business?''

I whirled around to see a six-foot, gray-haired, fiftyish man with a tough build and a tough face. He wore civilian clothes, a gun I couldn't see but knew was there, and a big grin.

"Peter Hardy! I'll be damned!''

"That's Lieutenant Hardy to you.''

"Congratulations. When did this happen?''

"Ten years ago, give or take.''

"Give or take, nothing. Bet you know the exact date and hour.''

He nodded, looking comically embarrassed for such a big guy.

"But can it really be that long?''

"All of that, and more.'' He became aware of the other officers trying to look as if they weren't staring at us. "Hey, guys, this is Kay Engels. I knew her when she was a brand-new baby reporter, and she wrote the best story in town on a case I was on. Even got all the facts right.''

"Of course I did.''

"No of course about it. Plenty of you reporters don't. That's why I talked to you and not them.'' He stopped and gave me a mildly suspicious look. "What brings you here anyway? As far as I know, all we've got going today is the usual mayhem. Nothing newsworthy.''

"It's not exactly a story, Peter, and I'm not exactly a reporter now.''

"Looks like we've got some catching up to do.'' He looked at his watch. "I've got to be in court in less than half an hour. Walk over with me?''

As we walked, we talked. I ended with "So now that I'm at a weekly magazine, I don't cover city news anymore like a reporter. It's longer pieces and more variety.''

"Yeah, I've seen the magazine. Lots of fluff, isn't it? A whole lot of nothing.''

"Yes, I admit it, but not *all* of it. And the fluff is a change from the old days, all murder and war and accidents.''

"Yeah, daily life in the big city. So if it's not a hot story, why are you hanging around a police station?''

I told him about Vera and her project, the vandalism and my car, and finished with, "So you see, it's partly personal and I want to stay on top of it.

I'm damned if I'll just let it go. Besides, I hear it might not be an isolated incident.''

He looked startled at that. ''How did you know? You been talking to the building owners?''

I'd lucked out. Now I knew Mr. Earl's story wasn't just gossip.

''No,'' I answered. ''Should I?''

''Jesus, no! They're already putting the screws to us. A reporter will really make them blow it way up.''

''Come on, Peter, what is it? I *will* start asking them if I can't ask you.''

He appeared to think it over before finally saying, ''There's been a little series of vandalism incidents at some of these big downtown buildings. Nothing serious so far.''

Before I could respond indignantly, he went on, ''Yes, I know you're upset about your car, but trust me, it could be much worse. There's been a lot of it, though, and it's expensive and annoying, and the building owners are up in arms.'' He ended, morosely, ''Of course they're pretty well connected, too, friends of the powers that be, if you know what I mean.''

''Sure. They're on your back. Who's investigating?''

''Kay! I'm not even supposed to have told you anything.''

"You didn't," I answered promptly. "I already knew from another source, remember?"

"Is that source anyone I might know professionally?"

"Doubt it. No, it's not a cop, okay? So are you going to tell me who's investigating, or do I have to find out on my own? You know I will; you could just save me some time."

"You're reminding me of why I don't like reporters."

"Peter, you're hurting my feelings. It's my car and my friend, after all."

"Hurting your feelings? Give me a break. A reporter on a story has no feelings. But, okay, you found out on your own, so what's the point of stalling you?"

"Cop reflex?"

"Right about that. Here's the guy's name and number." He wrote it on a card. "Give me a chance to call him and tell him it's okay to see you."

By then we'd reached the courthouse. "I gotta run. My number's there too. Keep in touch, kiddo. And good luck with the car."

"It was great to see you, Peter. Whoops, I forgot, Lieutenant Peter!"

It *was* great to see him, and lucky too, but I headed straight for a phone to call the number he'd just given me. I wasn't going to take a chance on my old friend warning his colleague not to talk to

me. In the great scheme of city life, vandalism
would have to be regarded by police as an ordinary
nuisance. Prominent and irate owners of major
property, however, might be a very large nuisance
indeed.

Peter's name got me a cordial response from the
right person, but he wouldn't tell me more than that
it was an ongoing investigation. I asked a lot of
questions, hoping I'd distract him enough to let
something slip. He was experienced and gave away
nothing except the admission that there was a small
problem in the area, nothing that would be of any
interest to anyone not directly involved. As this was
paired with the information that the investigation
was ongoing, I wasn't convinced.

I fed quarters into the phone, wondering if it
wasn't time to break down and get my own cellular
phone. I called Jerry Murtaugh and learned that
they had no idea what had become of the missing
watchman the other night. They had not heard anything from the police about the property damage
and the shooting. He was polite but, finally, dismissive.

"Miss Engels? I know you're upset about what
happened, but I've got a building to put up here,
and we're on a tight schedule. Every delay costs
money. You want to talk more, come around, say,
five o'clock. But unless something happens be-

tween now and then, I just won't have anything to
add.''

It seemed to me that he was surprisingly calm.
Was he just stonewalling me? Or was it that none
of his own company's property was actually destroyed? I was starting to look forward to seeing
what my friend in research would find on Carson
Construction, and I was already thinking ahead to
ways of digging deeper.

EIGHT

I HEADED FOR MY LAST subway trip of the day, a crowded one in rush hour. I'd just have time for a cool drink and a shower before Alan came to get me.

Since I had no idea where we were going, and it was still very hot, I settled on a short black skirt and bright silk sleeveless wraparound top. I thought it would be fine for almost any place, and when Alan walked in, I could see from his expression that he approved. This was beginning to feel like a date. I firmly suppressed any uncomfortable thoughts about that.

I watched him through the half-open bedroom door while I did my last-minute things. He roamed restlessly around my small living room. He looked over my massive, messy floor-to-ceiling bookcases, my main decorating theme, if you could call it that. My place certainly doesn't have that glossy, artful style that is surprisingly common in New York. At least, it's surprising to me.

He looked at the framed black-and-white photos on the walls, mostly taken by news photographer friends. I wondered what he thought of it all: the twenty-dollar flea market coffee table on the very good Chinese rug; the worn garnet corduroy sofa, the one item saved from my marriage. Could he tell it was a sofa bed, chosen to accommodate friends who turn up from any part of the world at any hour, on the way to or from assignments? Could he tell that the quilt hanging on the wall was an antique that I'd seen at a show, coveted wildly, and gone into short-term debt to buy?

When I emerged, fully made up and accessorized, he said, "Cute place. Very West Side." His expression was quizzical.

I laughed and said, "What? What is it?"

He shrugged and grinned. "It's cozy—no, I mean it—but I picture you somewhere very spacious, very elegant."

I didn't know if I was more surprised that he pictured me that way, or that he was picturing me at all.

The car double-parked outside my building was not the chauffeured limo that had taken us to the wake, but a red Miata convertible.

"Is this car as much fun as it looks?"

"Even more. Would you like to drive it later? Can you drive a stick?"

"What an insult! Of course I can. And I can drive a jeep, and I *have* driven small trucks, though I'll admit I'm kind of a hazard when I do. I haven't spent my whole life taking taxis, you know."

He laughed. "I did. I grew up in New York and

didn't learn to drive until I was in college. I've made up for it since, though.'' He moved the car smoothly in and out of traffic, never wasting a motion and never losing a moment to other drivers' hesitations or missed traffic lights.

"Where'd you learn to drive a truck?"

"A friend taught me when I was in the Middle East, years ago. He said I needed to be able to get around by whatever transport was available." I added, "I drew the line at camels."

"Did that come up? You're kidding!"

"No, it did come up a couple of times, and I did it, but only as a passenger. I've ridden donkeys too, and uncomfortable, smelly little beasts they are!"

He shook his head. "Amazing. I look at you, and I can't begin to take in what you've been doing with your life. I want to know it all some time. But right now, when it comes to transportation, don't you prefer this?"

"Over a donkey? No contest. Over my own car? Leather upholstery, silky smooth ride, push-button everything, over dead shocks and temperamental air-conditioning? Gee. I'll have to think it over." I looked around and was surprised to see that we were heading up the West Side Drive, away from the heart of the city.

"Where are we going?"

"The Bronx."

"What?"

"Wait and see."

When we crossed a small bridge just short of the Westchester County border, I said, "You conned me. We're going to City Island."

He smiled. "I resent the accusation. It is the Bronx."

"It's not usually what people mean. I know it's this little separate island out in the harbor, but I've never actually been here. What a fun idea."

"You'll like it. It's sort of a one-evening trip to Cape Cod."

It was true. We strolled the single main street, peering into the windows of the bait-and-tackle stores and speculating about the uses of the mysterious marine items we saw inside. We looked over the offerings listed in the window of a boat broker. When we passed a small gift shop, Alan said, "Wait here. You need a souvenir."

He came out empty-handed but grinning, and said, "It's a surprise. You'll just have to be patient."

The street stopped at the water, where the view was dominated by a sprawling seafood restaurant of the bare-feet-on-the-deck variety.

"Like any beach town! And it's right in the middle of the city."

"Exactly, but we're not eating here. Perfect after a day at the beach, with sand in your shoes and hair, but not quite right for tonight."

We turned away from the main road and walked on carless streets past modest homes. The sky was hazy and the stars as dim as they are everywhere above New York, but everywhere we went we could hear the water gently lapping, and the air smelled of the sea.

We turned at last into a huge brick restaurant, all dark-red-and-gold trim, elaborate chandeliers, and lots of mirrors, an outdated idea of elegance that I somehow found charming tonight.

The place was bustling, even on a midweek night in late summer, but we were soon whisked to a table for two next to one of the large windows looking over the dark water and the distant sparkling lights of the city.

"What do you think?"

"I'm actually tempted to get romantic over that skyline view, but what is it really? A housing project?"

"More or less."

"I should have known. Well, it may not be glamorous, but it's pretty from here, I must admit."

In no time a waiter was bringing us a basket of fresh Italian bread and an old-fashioned glass relish dish with celery, olives, and red peppers, while another waiter took our orders.

Alan urged lobster, the house specialty, but I ordered mine as a casserole. I was not about to wear a bib and wrestle with lobster crackers, spraying juices and melted butter everywhere.

He said, "There's nothing like the shore to help me unwind, so I hoped it would work for you too."

"Yes, it has. It was a great idea. I do feel as if we took a little trip right out of the city."

"I'm glad it worked. I wasn't sure if it just does it for me because I grew up on the beach."

"Did you grow up here? Didn't you say Manhattan?"

"Yes, but I started out in Brighton Beach, out near Coney Island. It was a little like this then, though much bigger. Now it's completely changed."

"It's very Russian now. Little Odessa, they call it."

"That's just the latest change, but back when I was a kid, it was still kind of a vacation community. Families from other parts of Brooklyn rented little bungalows in Brighton in the summer. There was a boardwalk too, with all the junky foods kids love: hot dogs with sauerkraut, knishes, corn on the cob. And huge waves on the beach, and gulls. It was wide open then, just huge sweeps of sky and beach. Living there was like being on summer vacation all year. For years after we moved, I hated going back. It was just too changed. Destroyed, really."

"I don't understand. What happened?"

"Block after block of apartment towers, and the

population doubled. Developers just buried the old neighborhood under massive construction and ruined everything that made it so great. It just disappeared under the concrete. For me, anyway.''

He shook his head. ''We moved to a penthouse in Manhattan when my father started making money. I was eight or nine. My folks thought it was moving up in the world, but I sure didn't. I thought it was more like—''

''Exile?''

''Yeah. I was really mad at my parents for a while. A long while.''

''Are you sure you aren't exaggerating the death of the neighborhood? I spent some time out there about a year ago. It seemed vital and even exotic, though, I admit, not much like a beach town anymore.''

''You in Brighton Beach? I can't picture it. What brought you way out there to deepest Brooklyn?''

''We did a couple of stories on a Russian immigrant who has a gymnastics school, and he and I hit it off in a strange way. He tries to get me to write more stories, and he worries about my life.''

''That sounds like Anatoly!''

When I looked surprised, he admitted, ''I know him. I've still got ties. Would you like me to take you out there sometime? Ever eat in a Russian restaurant?'' I shook my head. ''It's an experience; that's the only word for it. There's nothing else like

it. You shouldn't eat for two days before, and you
can't eat for two days after."

By then I was working my way through my lobster, after an enormous appetizer and a salad, and I
said, "I'm beginning to feel that way now!"

He laughed and said, "No comparison."

"So you loved Brighton Beach, and didn't like
the penthouse, and do like City Island. What's your
favorite neighborhood?"

"Great question for someone in real estate. The
easy answer is: anywhere I can make money. The
real one is probably that I like a lot of them for
different things. I like SoHo, where I live now."

I was surprised. I'd placed him on the Upper East
Side, post-prep-school, Brooks Brothers country.
SoHo is trend city, an old industrial neighborhood,
now filled with art galleries and cutting-edge cloth-
ing shops. It was renovated first by artists looking
for cheap large spaces with plenty of light, and then
renovated again into stylish loft apartments by people with money who liked to be thought artistic.

"I didn't have you as a SoHo type."

"Ah, but I'm in the real estate game, don't forget. I bought an old garment factory a long, long
time ago, just as it was becoming SoHo. Converted
it into loft apartments and made quite a nice profit.
That was actually my first development, when I was
still a lawyer."

"I had a feeling you weren't always in development."

"No, not at all. Dad sent me to the best schools, Fieldston and Princeton, thought I'd go for an MBA and bring all that Ivy League education back to the family business, but I had to stake out some independence." He smiled somewhat wryly. "I did fine as a lawyer, but I was always noticing neighborhoods, seeing trends, looking at buildings going up. When my wife and I split up, she took the brownstone, and I moved into my favorite loft. It's sensational. I'd love you to see it."

He leaned back. "Now let me guess about your little place. I bet you moved in way back, when West Side side streets had beautiful, run-down, cheap housing and you shared the block with drug dealers. You were probably too naive to be scared."

"How did you know?"

He shrugged. "I know neighborhoods. I know who lives in them too. The building front, and those French windows in your living room, tell me it was a beautiful home once. And your tiny rooms tell me it was badly chopped up into apartments. And even a tiny three-room place in that neighborhood gets top dollar now, but was dirt cheap—when?"

I laughed and said, "I'm not telling."

"That's another neighborhood that's changed a lot. What do you think of it?"

"It's a wash," I said slowly. "I always sublet

my place when I was overseas, and I was always stunned to see how much changed in a year or two. I don't miss the drug dealers. I do miss the little neighborhood stores, you know, the shoe repair place and dusty old hardware store. The first fern bar with good food and cappuccino was a sign of progress, but we don't need two on every block. The streets are safer now, yet there's still a kind of edge to the neighborhood, thank God.

"I guess I must like it. Even when I was married, I sublet my apartment instead of giving it up. My ex-husband once used that as proof I wasn't really committed to the marriage."

"True?"

"Maybe. I was glad to have it to go back to." I changed the subject quickly. "Tell me about your new building downtown."

"Where Vera's working?" He grinned. "I'd love to. It's my biggest project, much, much bigger than anything I've done so far. It's my real jump into the big time, a first-class office building, the best design, very elegant; the most up-to-date mechanicals, the top of the line in every way. It's going to put me right on the real estate map with all the big boys. I've been working my way up to this for a long time."

"Then it means a lot to you?"

"'A lot' doesn't even come close. Putting this together has been the biggest high in my career so far, but seeing it standing there, complete and perfect—well, that will be like winning the World Series.''

I smiled in an attempt to neutralize my next question. ''What's it like working with Vera? We're lifelong friends, so I know as well as anyone that she can be pretty stubborn.''

He nodded. ''She is that, but I can deal with it. I've known her a long time; we had friends in common and used to run into each other here and there.'' He paused. ''I pay for her work. Did you know that? I mean my firm, of course. I was glad to throw the job her way.''

''It doesn't interfere with the building?''

He shook his head. ''It would be good to get in there now, but we don't actually have to work there for a couple of weeks. I can afford to lose a little on this.'' He smiled somewhat sheepishly. ''I don't spread this around in construction circles, but I was an art history major in college. I took some ancient art courses, some anthropology, I'm on a few museum boards. I have to respect what she does. We'll make a nice lobby display with some of her finds; it'll be a classy finishing touch.''

''Art history? At Princeton?'' I asked about a famous architect who taught there, and from there we went on to talk about college experiences and the roads that brought us into our present careers. By the time we were done, we'd shared a gigantic strawberry shortcake, finished our wine, and walked out to the parking lot.

"It's a nice night. I think I'll put the top down, if you don't mind? Would you like to drive?"

"I'd love to! Do you trust me?"

He tossed me the keys, and I couldn't resist saying, "Thanks, Dad!"

There wasn't much traffic, and I did enjoy really letting the car out. We didn't talk much. I was concentrating on driving a strange car, and I suspected Alan might be holding his breath, watching me, but if so, he was tactful enough to hide it.

As we approached my building, he pointed to a garage at the end of the block and said, "It goes in there."

"All right," I said, surprised and a little wary. What was going on? Was he assuming this would be an all-night date? I was going to have to change his mind pretty quickly. When we stopped at my front steps, he said, "Here's your souvenir," and took from his pocket a key chain with an enameled disk that said, "City Island, The Bronx" on it. There was a set of car keys attached.

"The Miata's on loan to you until your car is fixed. I rented garage space for a month."

"What?"

He nodded. "I felt bad about your car, and I wanted to make it up to you."

"That's ridiculous! I can't take your car."

He made a dismissive gesture. "My own car is just like it, but it's in my garage. They're all leased by the company; we have connections; we get a great deal."

Was that true? I wasn't sure, but he stopped my questions with gentle fingers over my mouth. "Let me do this for you. You looked great in it, like you've never driven anything else." He smiled slyly. "And you know you loved it. Admit it!"

I had to laugh. "All right. I did."

"So where's the harm?" He wrapped my fingers around the keys. "I'll call to see how you're doing with it." He kissed me on the cheek and walked away.

I had been manipulated, and I knew it, but to what purpose? This wasn't officially a story, so I wasn't being bribed. Was it a new approach to seduction? An interesting thought, that was. Was it personal? Alan seemed very nice, and I had enjoyed our evening. Certainly he was good company. But no one becomes rich in a cutthroat business in New York by being nice. Or was he telling the truth, that he just felt some responsibility about my own car and was trying to make it up to me?

It was way too high-handed to suit my sense of independence. I don't like being taken care of. That's what I told myself. That's what I've been telling myself for a lot of years. Yet as I ran up the stairs, car keys dangling from my hand and jingling with each step, I wasn't so sure.

NINE

THE NEXT MORNING, an early call to the office research department told me that Nancy would not be able to get to my questions about Elkan's business, and Carson Construction, right away.

"Sorry, Kay," Nancy said, "but you know stories on deadline come first. I do have one little thing for you, though. Hold a sec." She returned and said, "Here it is, in the current issue of *New York Business,* an article on the new Elkan building downtown. It's short. I can read it to you. Or did you ever get a fax machine?"

"Yes, I just did. Give me a minute to figure out how to switch it on."

And in five minutes, a copy of the story was sliding onto my desk. Amazing.

It was largely a puff piece, describing how wonderful the building would be and what a comer on the real estate scene Alan was becoming. I skimmed it quickly until one brief phrase brought me up short. "Elkan, son Stan Elkan, a prominent builder in Brooklyn and controversial developer of Brighton Beach..."

I gasped out loud and sat down to reread the whole article again, this time with great attention.

There was nothing else, but that single phrase told me that Alan had lied to me last night. No, not lied, precisely, but certainly misled me, and I did not doubt that it was deliberate. The family business was not vague investments; it was real estate. And it seemed that a leading destroyer of the old Brighton Beach he loved must have been his father. And that his father was somehow controversial.

At that moment Alan began crossing over, for me, from being an attractive man to being the subject of a story. I expect story subjects to lie, or at least to shade the truth. Politicians, movie stars, athletes, they all have an agenda. I don't expect it of men in my personal life. Or at least I expect the lies to be about ordinary things, like other women. This was something else. I didn't like having a smoke screen blown for my benefit.

Nancy wouldn't have anything else from the published record until later today, or even tomorrow, but maybe my talkative friend Anatoly would like a visitor today.

I had first met Anatoly when I was sent to do a story on him, a soft assignment after a particularly grueling one.

"Here's a reward," my editor had said. "No stress. A change of pace from crooked politicians and drive-by shootings." He handed me a Russian name and a Brooklyn address.

"We might like to do a feature on this guy. He

runs a kids' gym, and all of a sudden, his little gymnasts are looking like possible stars. Sports doesn't have anyone, and anyway, we're more interested in a human interest angle. You know, 'Olympic Gold Grows in Brooklyn,' that kind of thing. Hang around a couple of days. Take a photographer. Nice change, isn't it?''

Anatoly Sorkin had turned out to be middle-aged, short, muscular, mustached, and voluble. He immediately offered me tea, coffee, or soda. "We have small kitchen, you will see, downstairs. I have Russian pastry, too, very good. No? So we have later. Now I show you gym."

He proceeded to tell me at length and with enthusiasm why he had come to America. "Always in Russia I have ideas how to build, but no one wants to hear. No one wants to know. Here in U.S., I take skills from here"—he held out his hands—"and here"—clenched his arm—"and ideas from here"—he tapped his head—"and bring all together."

He and his wife had slowly built up the gym, working extra jobs, saving, and borrowing. He'd learned to market his services, "like real American businessman," he said. "I know I cannot start with only future champions. I must build to it. In meantime, every child can learn a litte tumbling, get a little strong, get a little graceful. So I visit youth centers, Boy Scouts, Girl Scouts, invite them to come for discount rate. I have open house four times a year. I have birthday parties here, very popular. Fun for children, no mess for mothers.''

Then he admitted, ''I am little bit socialist still. For gifted child with no money, we find scholarship. The mother with mink coat pays full cost, and that gives a little extra for others. Only for the best I do this, because there is great pleasure—you know? satisfaction?—to help talent grow.''

His determination, his heart, and his hopes touched something in our readers, and that little story brought a huge response in letters. People wrote to wish him luck in his dreams for his most gifted students, to be able to say, as he put it, ''Look here, you great coaches, you Karolyi, you Nuno, look what gymnasts we grow in Brooklyn.''

A year later one of his pupils did win a national title, and we had returned for a joyous follow-up story. We'd kept in touch. Every so often he'd lure me out to the far end of Brooklyn for an enormous Russian meal at his home, or he'd call, just checking in fractured English to see if I was keeping up my fitness program when I traveled and that I was meeting only nice men. I sometimes felt I'd acquired a Russian grandmother. It was odd to suddenly have someone worrying about me this late in my life, but it wasn't often enough to annoy me. I even found it endearing at times.

A phone call confirmed that he would be delighted, and yes, he knew Alan. "I know father too. Is my landlord."

I LEFT THE KEYS to the new car in my desk drawer. I wasn't going to accept Alan's gift, favor, compensation, or whatever it was. In any case, the traffic report on the radio told me that today a car would only slow me down.

The temperature rose a degree with every stifling step I descended into the subway station, but the subway car was suitably freezing, and the trip was uneventful. About halfway there the train shot dramatically from underground onto elevated subway tracks, and I could look out over homes with porches and streets with trees, a peaceful corner of the city that seemed weirdly transplanted from my rural hometown. I saw the towers of Coney Island's rides in the distance.

"SO YOU ARE BACK, Miss Kay! I have nothing new to show you now, but you will come when children return? With photographer? I give you date. You will have a glass of tea now? Or fruit syrup with cold seltzer? Is Russian drink. Very good."

"Yes, that sounds wonderful." I had learned that on a visit with Anatoly, Russian hospitality could not be set aside. "And yes, give me a date to come back in the fall."

When he returned with the drinks and the calendar, he said, "So, you are curious about Elkans. They are my landlord, here, in this building, and most of my neighbors, too."

"Alan Elkan?"

"Yes and no. His father own building and most of block, but Alan used to help manage. Not so much, now. Too busy, I think, but people in his office do it. Father is not well."

"What kind of landlords are they?"

Anatoly shrugged. "Landlords are landlords. Give as little as can, take as much as can. No, Alan is okay, pretty nice guy. The old man was tough customer. He was—" He said a Russian word. "It mean 'gangster' but not for real, you know, like Godfather, just tough, hard. Cannot quite say in English.

"He own lots of neighborhood, and not too popular. I have many friends in his towers."

"Which towers are those?"

He looked surprised and pointed to where an enormous housing complex loomed over the low-rise old neighborhood.

"There. Those are all his buildings. Brighton Beach Towers. I know many people there."

So Alan's father had been not only a developer of the area but one who worked on a massive scale. The complex was as big as a good-size village.

"Could you introduce me?"

"Sometime, not now. All at work. But you

know, many people there are old. Like to sit on benches and talk and talk.'' He grinned. ''Talk to anyone, even reporter.''

I thanked him for the suggestion, confirmed our date for next month, and walked in the direction he pointed. As promised, benches lined the paths between the buildings, and they were filled with people hoping to catch a breeze from the ocean.

I deliberately slowed my purposeful walk to a weary stroll, and after sizing up the sitting groups from behind my sunglasses, I sat down next to one as if by chance. Easing the backs of my shoes off, I looked like any casual tired walker.

Next to me were three talkative elderly women surrounded by bundles and shopping carts. I turned to the one next to me and used that all-purpose conversation starter, ''Some hot day, isn't it?''

''Oh, honey, it is a scorcher,'' said the woman, who wore inconspicuous summer clothes but sported hair an astonishing shade of red. ''There would be more breeze over on the boardwalk, but we're just coming back from shopping and needed a little rest.''

''This weather's hard on old feet,'' one of the others said. ''Mine are swollen right up. I see you've got your shoes off too,'' she added, with the conspiratorial air of a fellow sufferer.

I smiled and nodded ruefully and asked, ''Where do you shop? I have a chance to take over an apartment in one of these buildings, so I thought I'd scout the neighborhood a little." I was trying to lead the conversation gently around to the subject of the landlord.

"Well, there's plenty of good shopping right on Brighton Beach Avenue," said the third woman, a fluffy blond in stretch pants that looked somewhat incongruous on her sixtyish frame. "And there's a fruit stand on every corner now. That's something the Russians brought in. They love fruit!"

"It's a strange thing," the woman with bad feet said, "to live in a neighborhood all your life and feel like a foreigner. Sometimes I don't hear a word of English on the street."

"Come on, Fay," the blond said. "Be honest. When we were growing up on Brighton Fifth Street, most of *our* parents spoke Yiddish. So what's the diff? Feels like when we were kids. And I like those Russian nightclubs." She stood up and did a little dance step.

This was interesting but was not telling me anything useful. I had to move the conversation in my desired direction.

"So what do you like about living here? And what don't you like?"

"It's the beach that makes it special," the redhead said. "There's nothing like the ocean. Otherwise, it would be just Flatbush, a real boring place."

"This one," the older woman said, "she isn't a native to Brighton, but she loves the ocean. Spends all winter in Florida near a warm one, then comes back to us to cool off in the summer."

"It's true. I could never live anywhere without water. And I swim every day. That's how I've kept my girlish figure." She said it with a broad wink.

"Oh, go on, you swim to meet fellas on the beach, just like Rose and me did when we were kids."

She grinned and shrugged. "So what if I do? I did the same thing on Lake Ontario when I was a kid. I'm not dead yet—and every once in a while I meet a man who isn't!"

They all cracked up at that. Once again, I felt lost in their good-humored banter. I would have to abandon subtlety completely.

"What are these buildings like? Well kept? Does the landlord do right?" I asked bluntly. "I can take a friend's lease, but I just don't know…" I deliberately let my voice trail off, hoping they'd step in.

"They're not what they used to be," the oldest woman said. "I've lived here since they were built, and I've just got to say it. Maintenance…" She made a dismissive gesture and a disgusted noise.

The others agreed. The apartments were nice size, nice layouts, but the landlord was too cheap to keep them up right.

"You wouldn't believe it, but my neighbor had

her ceiling fall down in her bedroom, just like that, and she was in bed when it happened!''

"No! You never told us that!"

She nodded significantly. "And it took that lousy Elkan three weeks—three!—to get someone to fix it.''

At last. I asked, so very casually, "Who's Elkan?''

"He's the landlord here. A real son of a you-know-what, if you ask me. Put up all these buildings and made a bundle out of it.''

"You know," the redhead said, "I always heard—this was before I lived here, of course—but I heard some of the money that went into this wasn't on the up-and-up.''

The other two nodded. "There were always rumors.''

"Yes, talk. Way back when, there was even an investigation. Nothing came of it, though.''

The ''controversial'' Elkan. I needed to know a lot more.

"When was that? And what was being investigated?''

"Let's see. I moved in in 1968, no, '69, the year my oldest graduated college, and the place was brand-new. So it was a year or two later. Do you girls remember what it was all about?''

"Not really," the blond said. "Something about funny business with the financing, maybe? But listen, honey, landlords are all the same, cheapskates one and all, even if they aren't crooks.''

"Do any of you actually know this man?" I asked, wide-eyed.

"Nope, I only deal with his agents, and they're no bargains either.''

"I met him once," the redhead said. "Walked right up to him at a meeting and told him what I thought.''

"That's right, I was there," her friend said. "And he just brushed you off, didn't he?''

"Of course. He called me 'little lady.' What does he care? But he is one mean-looking man, and nice suits and a flower in his buttonhole can't disguise it.''

"Not like that son of his. Now, he's a different type altogether.''

That got my attention.

"Oh, yeah. He spoke at a tenants' meeting one time. Nice young fella. Very respectful to everyone. If he was running this place—''

"He doesn't?" I said.

"Not really. He was filling in that time, when the old man was sick. He used to do that a lot more, but he's not around much now.''

The redhead nodded wisely. "I've seen his name in the papers. He's off building on his own. In Manhattan, no less.''

"Probably wants to make his own name. It's like

that in every family business, large or small. I remember when my brother David begged my
nephew Sammy to go into his smoked fish business
with him. I mean, *begged.* But no, Sammy had to
go out on his own, and guess what? After he sold
his own cheese business for a nice sum, he went in
with David after all.''

All the women nodded agreement and had their
own stories to tell. I could see that I'd learned all
I could, so I thanked them and left. The ride back
to Manhattan would give me time to make some
notes, but before I went to the train, I called my
office for messages. Alan had called and said he'd
call again later. There were a few unimportant other
messages. Vera called, saying only, ''Can't talk
now, but can you come to my place tonight to tell
me how we're doing?''

And finally my friend Marsha called from Miami
and said she had news. And in the heat of a New
York summer, on a steamy street corner, my hand
holding the phone went cold while my heart rate
doubled.

I couldn't return the call from an open pay phone
on a noisy street corner. I hurried on to the train,
thinking it would be faster than a cab, and occupied
the next hour by gluing my eyes to a book I carried,
reading intently and absorbing nothing. Afterward,
I couldn't even remember what book it was.

TEN

My FINGERS SHOOK as I dialed Miami. "Marsha, I got your message. What've you got?"

"Why, Kay, you sound awfully tense. Are you sure this isn't some big story you're stealing? You promise?"

"I promise, I promise. I'm just a little anxious. It's important to me personally."

"Okay, I get it. I won't pry. For now. And you know that is a major sacrifice for me."

"I know, and I will tell you all about it someday. Is that good enough? Now, what about that information already?"

"Hold those horses just a minute while I find it. Here it is. You asked me to find a Sally Ryan, born August 9... We've got a Sally Ryan Schwartz, same birth date, Florida driver's license, right here in Miami. Kay, are you still there?"

For a moment, I couldn't speak. Sally was a real person, someone I could call. Someone who could answer my questions. And she was in Miami. Marsha's town. A short plane ride away. I could hardly take it in. I finally pulled myself together, wrote down the address she gave me with a shaking hand, thanked her profusely, and said good-bye. I was so excited, I never even asked her how she'd done it.

I sat there for a long time, just looking at the piece of paper. Then I did something even I knew was odd. I added the information to the long list of crossed-out addresses in my mother's old book, bringing it into the present after nineteen years.

I looked at all the different places Sally had lived. Working backward, the last address was another place in Florida, but before that, she'd lived in two places in California, and before that, three different addresses in Las Vegas. I could see that she liked sunshine, but could I tell anything else from this? Had the changes meant she was moving up in the world or down? And weren't most of these towns the homes of racetracks? Did that mean anything at all, or was it just a coincidence? I had to stop myself. Here I was, trying to piece together the story of a life from tiny and very old clues, when I had the most current clue in my hand.

My hand reached out to the phone. I was sure that with a current name and address I could get a phone number, but if I phoned her, what would I say? Now that this had turned into real life, the many imaginary scripts I'd been creating seemed all wrong. Inadequate. Stupid, even. And would hearing from me be too much of a shock for her? I reached for the phone again, and again I stopped. I just couldn't do it. Finally I decided to go back

to my earlier approach. I took out the letter that had
been returned to me, addressed a fresh envelope,
and mailed it, fingers crossed, on my way to Vera's.
It crossed my mind that I had become like Vera,
digging back through the years to solve a puzzle.
Only, Vera was trying to reclaim a long-dead piece
of the city's life, while I was trying to get back a
missing piece of my own.

I was surprised, when I got there, to see that Vera
had a guest, a big, dark, good-looking man with
deeply shadowed eyes. It took me a minute to recognize Kevin Conley's father.

Vera introduced us again, inattentively, and Mr.
Conley continued the conversation my arrival had
apparently interrupted.

"So you see, we thought all this stuff here in the
box was yours, really, little things Kevin brought
home to show us from your work." He rested his
hand on the box on Vera's desk.

Vera nodded. "He liked to see what we were
doing, and he had lots of questions. Good ones, too.
He was so excited when he found a few things on
his own, and wanted to take them home for a
while." She shrugged. "Nothing valuable, so I said
sure."

"It didn't mean much to us. I mean, it looked
like old broken junk, no offense, except for those
couple of coins, but he was so excited. Said it all
meant something to them that knew what to look

for, and he tried to tell us a little.'' He swallowed
hard. ''Anyway, seems like this should all be
brought back to you, and I was coming into the city
anyway.'' His voice trailed away. ''There's an envelope in there with your name on it, papers or
something, too.''

Vera's expression changed subtly. Her visitor
didn't notice, but I knew she was surprised, and
hiding it.

''Do you want to open the box? Check to see if
everything's there?''

''Oh, I'm sure it is. Well, yes, all right, I will.''

It did look like junk, but it was all nested carefully in crumpled paper, and Vera touched each little item gently.

''We started our work in what turned out to be
the site of a privy, about three hundred years ago.
People used to toss all kinds of junk in them. It was
easy to find things. Kevin found these,'' Vera said
softly. ''See, this is part of a button.'' She touched
a dirty, whitish object, a rough, jagged half-circle.
''It's bone. When we clean it up, you'll see a design
on it. Someone threw it away when it broke. Maybe
it was smashed in a fight, or got caught in something.'' She touched some other undistinguished-
looking fragments. ''This is English salt-glazed
ware. It helps us date the site. You can just about
make out a design there. A blue-and-white might
be Dutch.'' She handed it to Mr. Conley and picked

up another white piece. "Now, I don't remember this," she said with surprise.

Conley nodded. "Kevin told us he found a few things on his own, one day when you weren't there. He never had a chance to show them to you, before—before—you know."

She shook her head, saying, "He shouldn't have been there without supervision, but I don't suppose he did any harm." She looked them over. "A bit of glass. More pottery." She picked up a larger white piece, saying casually, "This is a nice piece of a Dutch pipe." Then she turned it over, and her expression changed. "Kevin found this?" she said, with an odd note in her voice.

She turned on the bright light over her desk and took a small, soft brush out of a drawer. She brushed the object lightly, held it to the light, brushed it some more. When she turned back to us, she was breathing a bit hard and her eyes were bright.

"Kevin did a good job cleaning it. I just couldn't believe what—I mean, I couldn't believe what a good job he did."

She took a deep breath and turned decisively to Conley. "Thank you so much for bringing this to me," she said in a hard, bright voice. "None of this is extremely important, but it's all part of the picture, pieces of the puzzle, you might say, so I'm glad to have it back." She was easing him toward the door. "Please let me know if there's anything I can ever do for you. Don't hesitate to call me."

The minute the door was closed, I pounced. "What was that all about?"

Without a word, she handed me the fragment she'd been looking at, a curved piece of pottery, smooth, matte, and white. There were letters carved into it.

"K Y D. Kide? Kid? Kid. Oh, my God. Kidd. Is that it? Captain Kidd?"

She nodded, her face flushed. "Just a piece of trash," she said, stammering a little, "discovered in a garbage heap by an amateur. A kid with no training. And it proves everything I thought about this site."

"What does it mean, exactly, in terms of your work?" I said. "You're saying this really has to do with Captain Kidd, the pirate? A real live historical famous pirate?"

"Yes, yes, yes, I am! It wasn't actually his tavern, but I thought all along there was a connection. Listen, Kay, and I'll explain it all."

"And it's about time," I said, but she ignored me, her words tumbling out.

"Picture this. There were taverns all over the waterfront, and ship crews hung out in them then, just as they did all the centuries after, as long as New York was an active harbor. Just exactly like the old West Side, near the docks, when all the ocean liners and navy ships used to come here. One of those taverns, then, in the 1690s, was built by an old ship-mate of Kidd's.'' She took a deep breath and began again, more slowly.

"Let me back up. There was scarcely a differ-ence then between pirates, government-sponsored privateers, and regular ship captains. It was very fuzzy. The most respectable citizens invested in pi-rate ventures. Kidd himself *was* a respectable citi-zen for a while, married to a rich widow and active in civic affairs. He even helped build the original Trinity Church. When he was hanged, it was be-cause of politics almost as much as crime.

"Anyway, the crews might be precisely the low-lifes you'd imagine, but some were just poor men taking a chance on earning a stake. A couple of years of intense hardship on a pirate ship, and great physical risk, for a chance to get a share of fortune? To come home and buy a farm or small business, and be set for life? It was worth it for some who were really desperate.''

"Or really gutsy, don't you think? Kind of like gold explorers in the Old West?''

"Exactly. Only most of them didn't succeed even if they got the money.'' She shrugged. "Lacked the business know-how, missed the sea, missed the excitement, spent it all too fast. I don't know. But some did, and this particular guy— Greenfield was his name—did, at least for a while.

It's known that he operated a tavern for several years because his name comes up in written records, taxes and things, and he was involved in a lawsuit. Later his place burned to the ground, and he probably died in the fire. At least he disappears from the records after that. Anyway, he was an old shipmate of Kidd's, and they stayed friends. His place became the hangout for some of Kidd's crew. They drank there, did business there.''

"And what you've found is a tavern, and it did burn, and I assume the location is right?'' She nodded. "And now you have something to link it directly to Kidd. Wow.''

"It's a piece of a tobacco pipe. He must have kept his own there, a personal perk for the former captain. Who knows what else we may find about Kidd, or pirates, or just ships? Imagine it, Kay.''

And I did. A dark, smoky tavern. Dangerous-looking men drinking rum and paying with Spanish gold. A glamorous male figure with long ringlets and a great, plumed hat. A parrot on his shoulder.

I cleared my vision away with a sharp shake of my head. "I think I'm imagining a scene from *Treasure Island* crossed with Captain Hook. Get me back to this century, and *promise* me the inside story when you find it all. This is getting very interesting.''

"Yes, sure,'' she said distractedly. She was pacing her small apartment. "I know now this is major.

There's got to be a lot more there, and I just have to keep at it. And they'll just have to give me the time to do it." She paused and picked up the fragment. "I wonder if Kevin knew how important it was. I never told him anything about this." She responded to my questioning look.

"A little superstition, I guess. Don't talk about it before it's real. Besides, until I was certain, the fewer people who knew, the better. I sure didn't want the public looking for Captain Kidd's legendary lost treasure! And if it was as big as I thought, I wasn't taking a chance that anyone would try to take over my dig, either. That's happened."

An ugly thought was pushing into my unwilling mind. "Who *did* you tell? And who did you tell who knew Kevin?"

"When we were getting started, I had to do a little presentation for Alan, and Jerry Murtaugh, and a few others, about what we knew from research, what we expected to find, that kind of thing."

She looked at my grim face then, and said uneasily, "What are you getting at? What if Kevin told someone about what he found? Someone who did know it was important?"

"Vera, could your work hold up construction for a long time? If it did, would that cost the Elkans a fortune?"

She was as still and white as the pottery fragment in her hand. "Maybe Kevin didn't have an accident. Is that what you're wondering? Maybe Alan Elkan was protecting his investment?''

"I don't believe *that*." I had to say it quickly. I'd learned that Alan couldn't quite be trusted, but this was something entirely different.

"Why not? I'm having less and less trouble with it! Who else benefits? Who else could possibly be behind all this?''

"Alan didn't know Kevin. He told us."

"He said he didn't. That doesn't make it true. Or maybe someone was protecting his money for him.''

"It makes sense, but it doesn't. Vera, we're not talking tax evasion here. You *know* the man. Listen to what you're saying.''

She said with a twisted smile, ''No one really knows anyone, Kay. You've been a reporter all these years, and you don't know that? Alan has a nice surface, that's all. You don't know what's under it.''

She hit the mark with that, but I said, ''I think we're creating bogeymen here. Let's get a grip on ourselves.''

I wasn't about to consider, just then, whether my disbelief was an experienced reporter's hunch or something way too personal. I didn't want Vera to think about it either.

''Maybe there's more in that box that will tell us

something," I said quickly. "More artifacts? Wasn't there an envelope?"

I brought the box to her. She slit the envelope open and then dropped it with a startled exclamation. A handful of photos tumbled out. They were all of Vera. Vera in her apartment with a glass of wine in her hand. Vera on a blanket with a picnic basket, a Central Park bridge I recognized in the background. Vera in her office at the site, surrounded by books and tools, looking severely professional, and then in the same pose laughing, as if the second picture had been taken right after the first and the cameraman said something that cracked her up.

"Vera, what are these?"

"Oh," she said, visibly flustered, "Kevin liked fooling around with a camera. He brought one to work sometimes, took a few snaps of what we did." She faltered under my furious look.

"*This* is Central Park. *This* is your apartment. Cut the crap! I know romantic memories when I see them."

She started to cry, silently, eyes closed, head back against the sofa, tears sliding silently down her cheeks.

"I never meant it to happen. I told you. He used to hang around after quitting time, ask questions, try to do a little digging. He was fun, a cute kid, great body, very—very genuine. No pretensions, no attitude. No intellect or much education, but smart. You know? And eager. He was sweet. He was just a kid. Really a kid, too. Way less sophisticated than even my undergraduates.''

''You and I found the body of a man you were having an affair with, and you never said a word? Jesus, Vera, you are one cold woman! Why didn't you tell me?''

''I don't know! I don't know! It was all so stereotyped! You know. Professional woman of the world and young blue-collar stud. I felt foolish. And it really wasn't like that, no matter how it looks. I never meant it to happen. One night, we went out for a beer after working together. I mean, it was hardly a seduction scene. I'm a mess after a day at work, filthy and sweaty, and of course he was too. It got later than we thought, and he insisted on seeing me home. See what I mean? He was an old-fashioned sweet kid. And we were both a little drunk, and one thing just led to another,'' she admitted with some embarrassment.

''But when we found his body? Or after? With all that's been going on, how could you leave this piece out? We're friends, Vera. Friends share. How could you ask for—no, demand!—my help, all for the sake of friendship, and not tell me something this important?''

When she didn't answer, I said, ''Is this why you tried so hard to get me to help you?''

"No, Kay, not for a minute. I never even thought, until tonight, that it wasn't an accident."

"Can I believe you? I feel as if you asked me to solve a puzzle but you're hiding some of the pieces."

"Kay, it wasn't like that! Not at all. I was just trying to protect my chance to do my work. And in a way, to do it for Kevin, too. I never thought before there was a connection, but he was so excited by what we were doing—and he died there—I wanted to go on, somehow, for him."

She started to cry again. "I was so sure I knew what I was doing with him, and now I miss him much more than I ever thought I could."

"You were just trying to protect your work? Do you think my work means nothing to me? It means more than anything in my life. It is my life. It's the only thing that has ever worked out for me. How dare you play games with that?"

"If it was all that to you, then you know what I'm doing and why, Kay. You *know*."

"I don't know anything about you," I said quietly, suddenly too depressed even to shout. "I've been manipulated right from the beginning. You were using me. I expect that from politicians. I never expected to have to be on my guard with my oldest friend."

"But, Kay—"

"I don't know now if you're playing some kind

of deep personal game—or is it that publicity would protect your chance to finish your work? Did you invent a story to get me to provide it? The vandalism where nothing important is really damaged? Was that for real, or did you do it? And my car?''

"No, Kay!" She looked shocked. "I was desperate to assure that I had enough time, but I didn't do *that*. You can't possibly believe that of me. You can't."

"It seems I can't believe anything about you. You're on your own now. I don't even want the big story, if there is one."

I walked out the door.

ELEVEN

ALL NIGHT, two thoughts kept whirling around in my head: I had known Vera for nearly twenty years. I didn't know Vera at all.

I know a lot of other people whom I call friend. We talk, we laugh, we socialize, but there are few people I trust profoundly. Very few who are editors. Some other journalists, perhaps, but only if a story is not involved. Men, very few indeed, and I've paid dearly for trusting most of the ones I have. I liked Alan Elkan's surface well enough, but hadn't been fooling myself that I had a clue as to what lay beneath it. And I now believed he meant it to be that way.

I trusted Tony. There was no good reason for it, but I did, and it was probably for the same reason I trusted Vera: We went back so far together, back way before any of us had created the selves we had become.

And now I couldn't trust Vera. She had lied to me. And she had tried to use my profession to further her goals. It was the one thing in a friend I couldn't forgive.

All through the years, it never mattered that Vera and I could go months, and sometimes years, without seeing each other. We were busy pushing our careers along, meeting men, having adventures, gradually creating our grown-up selves. It never mattered. When we did get together, we could catch up, and then, if we were in the mood, leave our grown-up lives behind. Moan and complain, gossip and be catty, get silly, eat junk food with our fingers, harmonize with the Supremes.

Vera was such a small part of my daily life, really. I didn't know it was such an important part until I knew I had lost it forever. I was suddenly feeling very lonely.

My last letter from Tony hadn't helped the loneliness. He had written interestingly about his work, amusingly about Australians, sweetly about his daughters. He wrote about us, just a little, about how our adult time together had been so limited, he found high school memories floating into his mind.

It was a fine letter, but it left me unsatisfied. I certainly wasn't thrilled with the idea of Tony picturing me at seventeen every time he thought of me. Maybe I just didn't want a letter at all, but a shoulder to rest my head on, someone to confide in, someone to agree with me about Vera. Friend? Lover? Mother? I didn't seem to have any of those handy at the moment.

All of this was in my mind, but my body still went to work, and there the familiar rhythms and routines took over in spite of my preoccupations. I made calls and finished a story. I went to meetings. I fought with my editor. One day Alan called, and persuaded me to have dinner at his apartment by promising me a look at the building model and plans, and a chance to hear all the details. In spite of what I had said to Vera, I still wanted to know what was going on, and this would be a chance to ask a lot of questions. I told myself it was a working dinner. I didn't think of it as a date, and neither, I was sure, did he. And the warmth in his voice, and my loneliness, were not the reasons I rearranged my whole week in order to say yes.

When I arrived at Alan's building, he buzzed me in. The elevator opened directly into his top-floor apartment, an enormous sweep of odd-shaped, open space. The long wall was a row of floor-to-ceiling windows, a legacy of the days when this was a factory building.

"Amazing, isn't it?" Alan led me along the wall toward a central living space. Every window framed a different view of the downtown skyline at dusk. Three of the city's bridges, looking like gracefully draped spiderwebs, were visible from different angles.

There were no interior walls in the loft apartment. Counters defined a kitchen area; beautiful Japanese screens hid what I assumed was a bedroom space. A dining area was on a small platform. An enormous Oriental rug, thick and springy underfoot, with colors glowing in the sunset light, defined the living area. The small tables were marble, and the furniture was leather soft as silk. I had an overwhelming impression of being enfolded by luxury and taste.

"This is the best time of the day," he said, turning me gently toward the west-facing windows while the sky was turning into masses of deep blue and rose.

"I'll switch the lights on in just a minute, but for now, what do you think of this show?" Did I imagine it, or did his fingers linger for a minute on my bare shoulders, next to my sundress straps?

When the light at the windows began to fade, Alan moved to the wall, pressed a switch, and the enormous, shadowy space was instantly flooded with warm light from artfully placed fixtures.

"No, too bright," he said, and turned it down, replacing it by turning on a lamp like a sculpture that arced across one corner of the living area. "Drink?" He gestured to the table, already set with glasses and a bottle of wine.

As I settled into one of the luxurious sofas, glass in hand, and he sat on a low, elegant chair, he said with satisfaction, "That is how I picture you, in elegant surroundings, Steuben glass in your hand, St. Emilion in the glass."

"Why in the world would you see me that

way?'' He had said something like it before; I was just as baffled this time.

''You're a glamorous woman, Kay. Don't you know it? You look great, yes, but it's more than that. I look at you and I see someone with adventures, experience, a whole world of knowledge inside. Whatever you want to call it. True sophistication, maybe.''

I usually think of myself as a somewhat grubby working journalist. Deep inside, there still lives the unhappy, awkward teenager Tony remembered. I can do the glamour thing, but I never believe I fool anyone. I was so astonished at Alan's view of me that I immediately choked on my wine and had a coughing fit.

Alan came to my aid, and when I'd recovered, we were both laughing, and he had his arms around me.

''So much for sophistication,'' I said, laughing and gasping.

He said quite seriously, removing his arms but holding my hands, ''I think you're terrific.'' Then he seemed to take a deep breath, and said, ''How about dinner? It's all ready.''

I helped him take an elaborate meal of quail and risotto out of a suspiciously immaculate oven. In fact the whole kitchen, though equipped with every space-age appliance, looked as if it had never been used.

He saw me glancing around and admitted, "Yes, it's true, I don't cook, but I like good food, so I eat out a lot. I've gotten pretty friendly with some of the restaurant owners. They're usually willing to oblige with high-quality takeout when I'm entertaining. Just a cut above Domino's pizza, isn't it?"

He served the marvelous meal with considerable flair, and explained, when he caught me smiling, "Well, I've been watching the best professionals for years." Over dinner, he talked more about his project, bringing plans and drawings to the table to illustrate his words. I found myself fascinated by all the different skills brought into play, and by the sheer drama of creating such a tower, and by his enthusiasm. He poured more wine as he talked, a lot more, and by the time he was filling liqueur glasses with a sweet sauternes, I knew I'd had too much to drink. I made an effort to retrieve my professional intentions.

"Alan," I blurted, finally, "why didn't you tell me the other night that your father was a builder too?"

He looked sheepish. "How'd you find that out?"

"It's not exactly a secret, and finding things out is my job. Why did you try to keep it a secret from me?"

"I don't know. I'm not really proud of the old man. I hate what he did in Brighton Beach; you already know that. And I don't like what he puts up; it's ugly and cheap." His tone was becoming bitter. "I don't like the way he treats his tenants. I've been involved, a little, when he needed some help, and frankly, I don't want to be associated with him.

"You can do it with class and style, or you can still be a small-time Brooklyn operator, cutting every corner, no matter how big you get. And he did get big." He shrugged. "I guess I didn't want you to associate me with him. Maybe real estate is in my blood, but I don't have to be his kid. I can show him, and every one else, how to do it right."

"It's that important to you?"

He nodded. "I'll do whatever it takes. Borrow money. Fight City Hall. Negotiate every fine point in every contract." He was somber for a moment, lost in thought. So was I. Murderous ambition is usually just a figure of speech. I couldn't believe anything else just then. My discussion with Vera was strictly the result of high emotion and overheated imaginations.

"Let me show you," he said, helping me slide my chair out and deftly moving our liqueur glasses to the living area. He disappeared into a shadowy corner and came back with a model that he put on the table in front of me.

"This is it, just how the finished building will look. I brought it home from the office to show it off to you."

We leaned over it, and as he pointed out the miniature details, his hand rested on my neck and gently began to stroke it. It felt good. It felt wonderful. When he replaced his gentle fingers with his lips and a small tremor ran through my body, he put his arms around me, gently pressed me back on the couch, and began kissing me. I was way too willing.

"I'm drowning," he said finally. "I've felt this way since that first lunch, but I'm also not a green kid. I've got plenty of scars. Before I go under completely, I've got to know how you feel."

I stammered, "I like you a lot."

He looked stunned and said, "The kiss of death."

"No, no, I don't mean it that way. I'm so mixed up. There is a man in my life—"

He drew back. "Then why are you here?"

"Because he isn't. He's in Australia right now, and anyway, he lives hundreds of miles from here. It isn't exactly a relationship."

"Doesn't sound like impossible competition," he said, and moved closer again, one arm around me, the other hand gently stroking my hair, throat, face.

I was drowning too. By the time he had both arms around me, and his lips were on my mouth again, and my ear, and my throat, I knew that if I didn't grab that last overhanging branch, I was gone. And that branch had a large sign on it that said, "You are a professional reporter at work."

I moved a little away from him, took a deep breath, and said, "I can't, Alan. I like you a lot, and you know I'm feeling something here." I was feeling so much I was having trouble speaking. "But I'm on a story. Maybe. I mean, maybe there's a story about Vera's dig. You're involved; I can't be involved with you."

He leaned back and looked at me calmly. "Is there a story there? I doubt it. Did you come here tonight just to get information? Is this how you do it?"

I know I turned red at what he was so clearly implying. "No. I mean, it isn't how I work. I didn't think—I guess I didn't think we were more than acquaintances until—until tonight. And that's just exactly why I should go home now."

He nodded, his face still a mask. "That's okay. I do intend to keep seeing you, even if it's only in daylight, in a crowd, until you've satisfied yourself that there is no story and you know that Vera's leading you on a wild-goose chase. Be warned. I usually get what I go after." He stood and held out his hand to me. "Come on. I'll put you in a cab."

I adjusted my clothes, patted my hair, fixed my makeup, all without looking at him. He took me down in the elevator and waited with me to hail a cab and give the driver instructions, without once touching me or talking to me. Then he opened the cab door, and before I could get in, gave me a kiss that left my knees buckling.

All the way home, I thought about Alan's actions and how close I had come to responding. In fact, I was regretting that I hadn't. And it wasn't as much of a surprise as I was trying to tell myself, either. That same nasty little voice in my head, the one that reminded me I was on a story, not a singles cruise, was now pointing this out to me most unpleasantly. It asked me who I was trying to kid, and mentioned that I was way too experienced not to know the signs. And that I didn't usually wear a clingy jersey sundress and Shalimar for a dinner interview. What had I been thinking?

My personal and professional life seemed to be getting very tangled. In my tired, amorous, alcohol-fogged state, I was in no shape to untie the mess, but I knew I would have to find a way. Either I would tell Alan not to call again, or I would tell my boss there was no story after all. But too much had happened. I was convinced there was a story; I just couldn't figure out exactly what it was. I was damned if I was going to give up on it, in spite of what I'd told Vera in anger. In spite of the feelings Alan aroused. If there was something ugly to be dragged out into the light of day, I would do it. And not because Vera wanted me to.

TWELVE

When I got home, all I wanted to do was drop my clothes on the floor and lay my overtaxed brain on my pillow, but my answering machine button was flashing.

Curiosity, habit, or a sense of responsibility got the better of me, as they always had and probably always would. I pushed the button and listened as I undressed.

Vera's voice came on. "Kay, I know you don't want to talk to me, but I thought you might like to know there's going to be an important announcement at my site tomorrow at nine-thirty. My crew and I have been working every minute there's enough light, and we have substantial news. All the local papers will be there."

My body said, "No way; we're sleeping in." My emotions said, "We don't care. Vera is gone from our lives."

Nevertheless, at 9:25 the next morning, I was downtown, not exactly bright-eyed, sipping vile street cart coffee from a cardboard cup and chatting with an acquaintance from the Times. Vera appeared on the stroke of the half hour, looking pale and tired but composed, and passed out copies of a press release.

"Good morning. I am Dr. Vera Contas, archaeologist in charge here at the site of Elkan Properties' new building. In the course of a routine archaeological analysis, part of an environmental impact study, we have made some startling discoveries.

"Before giving you the background of this project, I'd like you to see for yourselves what we have found in the last few days. If you would just come this way, and be careful walking."

She led the small group to the digging area, where some of her student assistants were painstakingly brushing soil from what were clearly human skeletons.

A gasp went through the group. Vera held up her hands. "I'll be happy to answer all your questions. That's why I invited you, but perhaps it would be more to the point if I offer a few explanations first.

"This was the basement of a tavern that burned to the ground in 1698. It was probably owned by one Joseph Greenfield and was called the Lady Jane, after a ship he sailed on. We believed, from researching the historical records, that we would find the tavern here, and the archaeological findings confirm it. We found something even more dramatic than skeletons, at least to historians, related to the tavern ownership, which I will show you presently.

"As to what we have here, there are more questions than answers at this time, but what we are sure of is that there are at least two skeletons. We may find more. Both are male, and died, presumably, in the fire that destroyed the tavern. There are several obvious mysteries. The first is, Who are they? The second might be, Why did no one recover their bodies for burial after the fire? We can't answer either of those questions, yet, so I will tell you what we do know.

"One of them was poor. What remains of his clothes, such as buttons and buckles, are of the cheapest sort, roughly made of bone. There are tiny scraps of cloth that escaped burning; they look rough, too, but need further analysis.

"However, strangely, we did find a Spanish gold coin with a hole drilled in it, resting so close to his body it might have been on his person somehow, perhaps in a pouch or pocket that is now destroyed.

"Finally, we found a dagger with him, quite valuable, probably Toledo steel with a gold design on the hilt, and a jewel, perhaps a garnet or ruby.

"Here is where we found it." She pointed to his ribs. "Ladies and gentlemen, it is entirely possible we are looking at a murder three centuries old." She seemed pleased by the startled response of the crowd.

"The other skeleton is almost as mysterious. He appears to have been naked, or nearly so. He was shackled to the wall, and he died that way." She pointed to some links of a chain near the bones.

Then the questions came, fast and furious. Everyone wanted to know who the shackled man was. Vera answered, "He may have been a prisoner, though why he was here and not in jail isn't clear yet. He may have been a slave. It is possible to tell something about race from skeletal remains, and to my eye he looks African, but we will need a specialist to determine that."

"About the dagger," someone said. "When will you know if the guy was killed with it? Is it something you can know?"

"Yes, we can and will establish, from marks on the bones, if he was actually stabbed to death with it. We will be having a forensic anthropologist joining our team this afternoon, and we hope to start answering some of these questions with his expertise."

"Do you have any guesses about why the bodies weren't recovered?"

"There were heavy beams that collapsed in the fire, so perhaps it was too dangerous. Then again, maybe nobody knew they were there. Or cared."

"You said there's more to show us?"

"Yes. If you'll come back to my office now."

When everyone had gathered just outside her office, Vera began again. "Briefly, Joseph Greenfield was a former pirate who had sailed with the famous Captain Kidd, made some money, and settled down. He ran a tavern successfully, but apparently was nostalgic for his sailing days. We've found several items with rough carving saying, 'From ship Lady J.' More important is this item." She approached the group with a box in her hand. I recognized the object in the box as the bit of pipe I had seen in her apartment.

Vera said, "You are looking at a fragment of a tobacco pipe with Captain Kidd's name on it. We found it in a garbage heap, where it must have been thrown when it broke. It establishes without question that this was the Lady Jane tavern, which is known to have been a favorite of Kidd's."

"Wasn't Captain Kidd the guy with the legendary treasure? The fortune they never found, that people are still looking for?" one of the reporters asked.

"The one people have been digging all over the East Coast for, these last three centuries? That treasure? It's a glamorous legend, but most historians doubt there ever was a treasure, let alone a buried one. The idea got started because when Kidd was arrested, they never did find all the loot he was known to have had, so of course he must have buried it somewhere. After all, isn't that what pirates did? Well, they didn't. That's a legend. They were in business for money, and they wanted to spend it.

"Certainly, if Kidd had any surplus, he didn't bury it, and—this is terribly important—he didn't leave it in the hands of a powerless and relatively poor old shipmate like Greenfield. He had quite powerful friends, including the Gardiners of Gardiners Island. He would have used someone like that as a secret banker. Please don't write something that will send treasure seekers destroying what is the real treasure here, irreplaceable historical records! A great writer of historical fiction once said we shall never know ourselves until we have taken a long look back along the rocky road that brought us where we are. As New Yorkers, we are looking now at a completely fresh piece of that road.

"Unfortunately, we are working under intense time pressures, with only a week to go before Elkan Properties will be allowed to come in with the bulldozers, destroying everything here that could teach us something new about our beginnings as a nation. We may not have enough time to solve some of the fascinating mysteries raised here." She paused. "Unless, of course, the Landmarks Commission holds up the permit for this part of the new building. I am convinced that this site is significant enough to warrant such strong action. I am determined to convince the commission, and of course I welcome any help. Those skeletons deserve names and graves.''

At the end of the conference I turned to leave with the others, but Vera called to me.

"Kay, wait," she blurted out. "I did it, didn't I? I finessed them, Alan, Murtaugh, all of them."

"Looks like it. And without pulling my strings, or anyone's."

"Kay, I'm sorry. I didn't mean—I didn't realize—Look, I should have told you everything. I know that now. I didn't at first, because I felt a little foolish. I've sworn so many times I wasn't going to get into any more dumb involvements. Remember last time? I swore off men forever and said I'd live for work. And you didn't believe me?"

"I believe my exact words were 'When pigs fly.'"

"So I couldn't tell you. I felt stupid. And then when Kevin—when Kevin died—I thought you wouldn't help if you thought it was just personal. I was afraid you'd think I was overreacting because of Kevin."

With the previous night on my mind, I couldn't look straight at her. Finally I said, "How many dumb relationships have I slipped into since you've known me? Including my marriage. If it was a contest, I'd win." Then I did look at her. "It was manipulating my professional life that made me so angry."

"I know," she said in a small voice. "After this morning, can you sort of see why I had to do it? This is so important. Trying to get your help wasn't about Kevin. I didn't even connect the two until the other night. It was just exactly what I told you. I'd do anything to finish this, even use my oldest friend. And hurt her. It's that important. But I didn't lie to you about it."

I thought about my own secrets, my recent tangle of work and romance, and about Tony, and I knew I couldn't stay angry indefinitely. I wasn't as right as I wanted to be.

"Let's just forget about it," I said abruptly. "I'll get over it, but you owe me. I want an exclusive interview for my story, okay? You'll save *all* the best details just for me?"

Vera nodded. "Of course. Now?"

"No, I've got to run, but I'll call you tonight."

"Kay," Vera said as if she hadn't heard me. "What do you really think about Kevin? Were you—were we—serious the other night? It seems ridiculous in the light of day. Impossible. But if we were serious, shouldn't we be doing something? I don't know what. I've had so much to do here, I couldn't even find time to think about it."

"I don't know if I believe any of it either. No, I don't believe it, not really, but something isn't right. Something. I do have an idea about who to talk to, an old friend in the police department. Let me run it by him, just informally.'' She nodded, already looking over my shoulder, checking the work going on behind me. ''Now I've really got to run.''

Back at my office, Howard agreed that at last we had a story to tell.

''Captain Kidd? That would be the angle to play up. And can you get us a picture of those skeletons? Nothing sells magazines like bones. This is where you found that young guy dead, isn't it? And the vandalism? Now, that could be an eye-catching angle. You know, 'Haunted site. Pirate captain's revenge?' with a big question mark.''

I gave him a look that should have sent him straight to join Captain Kidd, wherever he was. He only responded, ''Yeah, yeah, I know it's corny, but readers love that stuff. Go ahead, write us a great story that will sell magazines. Interview your friend. Get background and pictures. We'll use what we can. Of course, no guarantees on how much space we'll have. Go. Write.''

I'd want some of the history for a sidebar, and I'd need it fast. Maybe Nancy could find me an expert to interview. And of course, send a photographer down there. And fill in every interesting detail with Vera that I didn't already have. I had a story to get together, but my interest in the problems at the site didn't stop there. I was going to call my cop friend, but before I did, the interoffice mail was delivered, and it included the results of my research request on Elkan's company and Carson Construction.

On the whole it was disappointing. Both companies were privately owned, and there wasn't much beyond announcements about various projects. For Carson, that was all.

For Elkan, there were a few articles from the local press, interesting but trivial, and not adding much to what I already knew, but at the very bottom, there was one extremely interesting piece. A report on the company showed that a substantial investor in Alan's company was S. Elkan, Inc. Alan's father. Another tidbit Alan hadn't chosen to share with me.

I called Nancy and asked for more, rush, please. Everything on Stanley Elkan they could get, and going back as far as the building of the Brighton Beach Towers in the sixties, if possible. I hoped they could get it to me before I left the office that night. Then I finally called Peter.

"Hi, Kay," he said. "Glad you called. Didn't know if I'd get to you today, but I've got news. We got the guys vandalizing those downtown buildings. Caught 'em red-handed last night. I think your friend can stop worrying."

"Tell me all. Who, why, the works."

"Don't know yet. They're just kids, there's three of 'em, and they're not telling us a thing so far,

stupid punks, but I guarantee they will. We wasted
a lot of department time and manpower on this.
We'll get answers.''

I wondered how he planned to do that, but
thought it wouldn't be politic to ask.

"Anything specific about Vera? Or my car?''

"Nope, not yet, but call tomorrow. All we know
is that they did it.''

"Will you tell me everything when you know?
And can I ask your expert opinion on something
else?''

I told him all about Kevin, whatever I knew, and
what Vera and I had discussed.

"Well, Kay,'' he said, "you covered crime for a
while. You must know there's nothing much there.
Unless you've changed a whole lot, it's not like you
to see bogeymen in the dark.''

"I know, I know. And maybe that's all it is. I'd
like it to be. Hey, my editor thinks it's Captain Kidd
taking revenge on the living!''

He laughed and said, "Get outta here!''

"Okay, maybe he doesn't think it. Maybe he just
thinks it's a good angle. But, I just keep wondering
if everything is what it seemed. Could you just take
a look at the records on Kevin's death and tell me
what you think?''

"Yeah, I could do that, when I get the time. You
know it's ninety-nine percent there's nothing
there?''

"I do know, Pete, but if there's that one little doubt— Thanks a lot. Can I buy you lunch next time I'm downtown?"

"Anytime, kiddo. Call me tomorrow, or the day after. Maybe I'll have something for you on those punks."

That night Vera's office shed burned to the ground.

She called me at 3:00 a.m., sobbing. After we talked a few minutes, I knew I would be writing a different story. The firemen had already found an empty kerosene can at the fire.

"That bastard," Vera was saying. "That bastard! He wants to scare me away. After today, he knows—he knows—he has to cooperate with me now. Kay, I don't know about Kevin, but this is deliberate. I'm going to get him for this."

"You mean Alan?"

"Of course I do. Who else? Who else would do this to me?"

"Vera, can you calm down? Back up and tell me exactly what happened tonight."

"No," she answered furiously, "I can't. I'm not calm enough—damn him!—but I will be. Talk to me tomorrow. I'm going to have a very large Scotch, maybe two, and go to sleep. Don't call me in the morning. I'll call you."

She hung up abruptly, and I was left to a sleepless night, rewriting all my notes, trying to make them add up a different way.

THIRTEEN

I ARRIVED AT THE OFFICE with a list of things to do: call the fire marshal's office; try to interview the firemen who were there last night; talk to Jerry Murtaugh (and wouldn't he be happy to hear from me again!); track down and talk to night watchmen in nearby buildings, again; and pry some money loose from Howard to pay for an investigation into Alan Elkan's financial affairs, the complex structure of his deals, and so on. This would require the services of a specialist, a researcher expert in financial investigations.

And call Alan. Yes. Call Alan. How many other things could I do before that was the only thing left, and I couldn't avoid it anymore?

IN THE END, he called me. "I meant what I said, Kay. I haven't given up, and I'm not going to. How about dinner tonight?"

"I can't, Alan."

"Okay. How about tomorrow night? Or we could go hear some music, if you'd rather do that."

"I can't do either one. I meant what I said, too."

There was silence for a moment. "I get the message, but I'd just like to talk to you once in a while.

How about lunch? That's businesslike and professional.''

"It's professional only if I pay. And only if we talk about the fire last night. And I don't have time for lunch, anyway.''

"Suppose we take a lunchtime walk in the park? Broad daylight and crowds of people? And you can buy me a hot dog? I promise I'll answer your questions.''

I agreed, finally, to meet him at one o'clock, and I went back to my calls. I battled with Howard, who agreed to some money for a financial investigation, not enough, but a start, and then the morning mail came in.

Right on top was my letter to my mother, stamped Return to Sender—Not at This Address. I'd used my office for the return address, thinking that if I were sent out of town, a reply could sit in my home mailbox forever, but if it went to the office, it would be sent straight out to me wherever I was. So there it was, a non-answer again. I flinched but slipped it into my attaché right away. It would have to wait. I was too busy today to think about my next move, or my feelings.

There was also a stack of clippings from the research department, very old stories copied from microfilm. The attached note said, "I had to apply pressure to my friend at the *Daily News* to get these. Are they what you needed?''

Oh yes, they were, a long series of items with screaming headlines and enthusiastic innuendoes, reporting charges and countercharges in the building of Brighton Beach Towers. Stan Elkan had financed the Towers with mob money. Or Stan Elkan was an upstanding businessman, a credit to New York. Stan was skimming public funds for the project into his own pockets. No, Stan was a cruelly slandered public benefactor, providing desperately needed housing for the neglected middle classes.

There had been investigations, committees, battling local factions, but as far as I could tell, nothing had ever been proven. And yet there was an awful lot of smoke if there was no fire whatever. And in the *Times'* more temperate account, something about the warring parties' characters and motives came across. I'd bet on the accusers.

I met Alan at Columbus Circle, and we strolled through the park toward the boat pond. The hot dogs from a cart were juicy, garlicky, greasy, loaded with mustard and sauerkraut. Perfect.

It was a perfect late summer day, too. The park was full of careening skaters, children eating ice cream, executives strolling in shirtsleeves, jackets slung over shoulders; sunbathing teenagers.

I looked at the handsome man beside me and steeled myself to ask reporter questions.

"Tell me about the fire last night."

He frowned—a worried frown, not an angry

one—and told me the facts, all of which I knew. I made sympathetic noises, and he said, "Damned if I know what's going on. I've never had a project with this kind of vandalism. And it's so pointless. Is Vera scared? It looks like she ought to be! At this point I'm really worried about her."

She's worried about you too, I thought. Aloud, I simply asked, "So you think it's directed at her?"

"Certainly seems to be. I wonder what enemies she's made. She can be—" He paused, then said carefully, "difficult."

"How about you as the vandal?" I said it deliberately, trying to see if it would shake him.

"Me?" His expression was a mixture of affront and astonishment, and seemed quite real. Could he be that good an actor? "Me? Where could you have come across a crazy idea like that?"

"Because if Vera's work slows down your building, it could be a very big and expensive problem for you."

"Kay." He stopped and put his hands on my shoulders, turning me toward him. "Look at me. Do you have any idea how much a building like mine costs?"

I shook my head. I didn't, but I would soon.

"Do you have any idea what a tiny piece of it Vera's work is, and how easy it is to work around her? Do you think I *want* this kind of publicity associated with me? After everything I said about wanting to do a first-class building?'' He let me go and we walked on. ''That is truly one of the dumbest theories I've ever heard.''

I said nothing, hoping he was right, but also wondering what he might say to fill in the long silence. It's a useful technique at times.

''You know,'' he said slowly, ''thinking about publicity, I wonder if there isn't someone who does benefit? Could Vera somehow be doing it herself?''

''How can you think that, after last night?''

''I know, I know, it's far-fetched, but think, Kay. Once again, no one saw anything, and no real harm was done. Strange, isn't it?''

I didn't admit that the same thought had crossed my mind. ''Alan, someone shot at her!''

''She *says*. No one else was there that time either. I'm sorry, Kay. I know she's your friend, so maybe you'll hate me for saying it, but there it is.''

''This is crazy.''

''It is crazy,'' he said in a hard voice, ''but *I'm* not crazy. Someone is screwing around with my project—maybe not Vera—and someone will pay for it. If pressing the police doesn't get results, I'll hire a detective on my own.'' He stopped suddenly, and said in a different voice, ''Oh hell, Kay. Here I am in the best park in the world with a beautiful woman and we're talking about vandalism!''

I felt a brief flicker of guilt at using his interest in me to get information. I suppressed it quickly.

"I'll change the subject," I volunteered. "How does the father you dislike happen to be a major investor in your business? And if you think so little of him, why are you using the family name for your business, just as he did?"

When he frowned this time, it was definitely anger. "So this really is a business lunch? And I'm an interviewee under the bright lights? I don't have to discuss my personal life with you!" He steered me toward the nearest park exit. "I'll find you a cab and say good-bye as soon as possible!"

It took us a few minutes to reach the gate, and as we approached it he said quietly, "I'm sorry. I think I gave you the right to ask anything you want to the other night. That just happens to be a touchy subject." He took a deep breath. "He offered the money. That's it. I never would have asked. It's a straight-out business deal, he has no control, and the terms are better than the bank's. Why not use him? And I used our name on purpose. I'm going to turn it around and make it stand for something very different in New York—first-class buildings instead of sleaze."

He spoke convincingly, and I wanted to be convinced, but I knew I wasn't, quite. By then we were at the street. Once again, before I got into the cab he kissed me so thoroughly I had to fight hard not to kiss back.

"When will I see you again?" he whispered in my ear.

"Don't know," I stammered. "I—I'm going out of town, I think. I'll call when I get back."

He kissed me again, and I was shaking when I got into the cab. As soon as I returned to the office, I went to see Howard. I said, without preliminaries, "I have to get off this story."

"What? This morning you had to have an investigator!"

"I do still. I do. I mean, the story does, but Howard, I just have to let it go. I'll turn all my notes and contacts over to someone else."

He looked skeptical. "This isn't you. What gives?"

"I'm too involved. I know too many of the people too well. My objectivity is shot."

He gave me such a long, considering look that I wondered what telltale signs he was picking up. Smeared lipstick? Tousled hair? Was I blushing, for God's sake?

Before he could ask me any more questions, I blundered on. "I want to take a few vacation days, too. I have plenty coming. I need to take care of some personal matters. Out of town." I'd made a spur-of-the moment decision to turn my lie to Alan into the truth.

"Kay, are you running away from something?"

"Yes." And proud of it. Let Alan and Vera make

themselves crazy suspecting each other, but I was getting out of it while I still had my sanity.

"Are you okay? Not in any trouble?"

I relaxed a little at that. "I'm fine, Howard." Maybe not fine, I thought, but not in trouble. Getting out of it, maybe. "I just have something I need to do."

He nodded. "Okay. Get your story notes together and see me before you go. And leave a phone number."

I went to my desk, called the travel department, and booked a flight to Florida. Six hours later I was getting off a plane. I spent the night at an airport hotel, and I was walking out the door the next morning at eight.

MIAMI WAS HOT. After the ferocious air-conditioning in the hotel, the intense outdoor heat felt wonderful for about thirty seconds. Then I began to feel it suck energy from me with each step I took toward the cabstands. I don't know how people stand it, and I didn't have to stand it for long. In just a minute I was inside a ferociously air-conditioned cab, speeding toward the *Herald* offices. Marsha had persuaded me to meet her there.

When I had called last night to ask for advice about finding the place, she insisted that I would not get one more piece of information out of her until I told her what was going on. I did finally tell her. It even felt good to tell someone about it. I couldn't help thinking about how often I'd used that human impulse to get people to talk to me, how often against their own better judgment.

She had been instantly intrigued and began describing a dramatic meeting, with dramatic headlines to go with it. I told her I'd cut off her typing fingers if my story was ever turned into a news item. Once that was understood, I could accept with gratitude her proclamation that I'd never find the place myself and she should take me there.

She greeted me with a big hug. Her hair was a new shade of blond, but her bright tropical clothes and unique voice were just as I remembered. Twenty years in Florida had laid a hint of the South, and Spanish expressions, over her original New Jersey accent.

"Honey, it is great to have you here! You look terrific, but just a *bit* frazzled. Did the heat get you? Come on, let's go get an iced tea, or a Coke, to revive you, and you can drink it in my car."

She swept me off to the soda machine, the garage, and into her convertible, and soon we were winding our way out of central Miami and heading off to some suburban district. There were large malls and strip malls and suburban subdevelopments. It looked a lot like Long Island with a trimming of palm trees and Spanish-style architecture.

After some prolonged wandering in winding suburban drives and culs-de-sac, we found what seemed to be the right area, a neat development of attached town houses, set off by an entrance gate with an office next to it.

"I think this is it, Kay. I don't think I've ever been out this way, but it's hard to tell. These places are a lot alike. Do you want to do it alone, or should I come in with you? You know I'm dying to!"

"Thanks, Marsha, for everything, but I think I'll go it alone."

The woman behind the desk was sixtyish, deeply tanned, wearing a pink muumuu embroidered in green and turquoise and pink rubber sandals. She looked up with a smile and said, "Now, let me guess! Nice young lady with no suntan. You've come from up north to visit an elderly relative, and can't make head or tail of the layout of the place. Don't be embarrassed. It happens all the time. I'm glad to help."

"I'm glad to hear that," I said, "but my question is a little different." I took out the letter that had been returned to me. "I'm trying to find this long-lost relative." How odd it felt to say it. "This is the only address I've been able to find for her, but I guess she's not here anymore. I just wondered if you ever knew her, or if you kept any records, when people move away, or—or—whatever."

"Pass on, you mean? I know it's hard to say, talking about loved ones, but after all, most people in these condos are pretty old. It has to happen, natural part of life, and yes, I might have records. Just let me get my glasses on.'' She fumbled with the ribbon around her neck, pulled her glasses out from her ample bosom, and put them on.

''I'll be!'' she said. ''How did this happen? It must have been that flighty gal who took over when I had my gum surgery.'' She slapped the letter, making an exasperated face at the same time. ''She hasn't moved out! She just goes back north for the summer. And who can blame her?''

''Do you actually know her?'' I couldn't quite believe the implication of her words.

''Of course I do. Lived here since the place was built, with a real nice, real elderly man. Oh, it's more like a housekeeper-companion setup, you know, not a romance, though we have some of those too, of course. Don't believe you're ever too old to fall in love. Sure, I know Sally, and she's a very nice woman, too. Now, this letter should have just been forwarded straight to Brooklyn.'' My expression must have given something away, because she said quickly, ''Honey, are you all right? Have a seat here.''

I was happy to sit down. I have never fainted, and I wasn't about to then, but the news did leave me a little breathless. She continued to eye me with concern.

''Bet it's the heat. It gets you if you're not used

to it, and I can tell you're a northerner. Here, let me get you a drink of water from the cooler.''

I drank gratefully while my informant rummaged in her desk. "Here it is," she said, "my list of forwarding addresses for the snowbirds. I know it's Brooklyn." She flipped pages. "Got it, but you know," she said slowly, "I'm really not supposed to just give it out to you. I don't actually know who you are or what you want."

I smiled my most disarming smile. It often worked. "Do I look dangerous?"

"Nope, but I still don't know you. You could be a process server, or some relative she doesn't want to see. We have a rule about this. I can't tell you where she is, but I can send the letter out again, right now, and let her decide for herself. Fair enough? I'll even put the postage on it."

And as she carefully copied the address from her book, I read it upside down and memorized it. I thanked her, practically ran back to Marsha's car, and wrote it down before I could forget it. "I can't believe it!" I said to her. I felt like giggling. "I can't believe it. Look at this."

"Goddamn!" she said after glancing at my notebook page. "She's been right there in the Apple all along. Amazing."

"I don't recognize the address," I said, "but I can find it on a map as soon as I get back."

"And when will that be? Something tells me right away."

"Oh, yes," I said. "I'd love a visit, but I am so anxious to follow this up."

"I know," she sighed. "Like a story, only more so. Well, if I'm not mistaken, the last flight to New York is about nine forty-five. We probably have enough time for dinner on the Beach. What do you say?"

I didn't want to pass up a chance to visit with Marsha, and couldn't pass up a chance to see the famed, revived, newly fashionable Beach district, so I said yes, and Marsha had me on the last flight home, as promised.

I HALF-DOZED, and the bright lights miles below the plane merged into a half-dream with bright lights from my childhood, the colored lights that lit up the fountain in the town square at night. My favorite treat when I was very small was to be taken downtown for a ride to see it in the night, way past my bedtime.

Sally took me one night, I thought. Memories suddenly flooded back, like scenes in a movie. It was our secret. She slipped into my room with a finger at her lips warning silence, her eyes laughing. She helped me into a sweater over my pajamas and slippers over my pajama-covered feet, and we tip-toed out the back door into the summer night. We both smothered our giggles as she carried me to the car.

Downtown, she parked, and we walked right up to the fountain, which I had never done. The water sprayed us, and we held our hands up and watched them turn different colors in the lights. Then we went out for hot-fudge sundaes. I could taste them in my dream. I was exhilarated by the strangeness of sitting up late at night in a coffee shop in my pajamas.

Mom and Dad were so mad when we got home…I drifted and came back with a start at the sound of the pilot's voice. Had I been dreaming or remembering? Did I remember raised voices after I was put to bed? Was that Sally's last visit?

I GOT OUT of the plane into the eeriness of an airport almost shut down at 1:00 a.m. By 2:00, I was peering bleary-eyed at my map of Brooklyn, not believing that the address I was looking for seemed to be somewhere around Brighton Beach.

I slept late, and didn't turn on the news radio until after I showered. It was well into the morning before I learned that sometime in the night someone had shot and killed Alan Elkan.

FOURTEEN

I SPILLED an entire mug of coffee over my hand and down the front of my blouse. I didn't even know I had burned myself until I saw the skin on my hand turn red. My mind told me I must hurt, but I didn't feel it yet.

I was waiting for the radio news to recycle in twenty minutes, because I did not believe what I had heard. I must have misunderstood. I waited in my wet silk blouse with a spreading coffee stain until I heard the story again, and knew that it was true.

They had only a few details. His body was found in his office by a member of the cleaning staff. There were no signs of a struggle or break-in. And the police were pursuing the investigation.

I didn't know what to do with myself, with my shock, my grief, and my questions. I poured another mug of coffee and then forgot it on the kitchen counter. I wanted—no, needed—to know more, and my mind was racing, thinking about whom to call and what to ask.

I found my coffee, poured a shot of brandy into it, and gulped it down cold. I stood staring out my window, mechanically counting passersby. I don't know how long I was there. I stopped when I realized my vision was blurred. My eyes had filled with tears, and they were running down my face.

Even if my mind had shut down in shock, my body knew how I should deal with it. Just as I always did. Apparently without my volition, it went to the phone, punched in Howard's number, and told him I wanted to be back on the story, and not to even think of saying no. I had to be back on it. It would be a much different story and I was the only one to write it.

I didn't even remember what he said. I'm not sure I even heard it. He may have been annoyed at my dithering. I didn't care. I changed my coffee-stained clothes and went to work.

I called Peter, who said, "Kay, don't even try. I don't know anything, and if I did, I couldn't tell my own wife, let alone a reporter. Not even you."

"Peter," I whispered, barely able to control my voice, "he was a friend of mine. A good friend."

There was silence. Then he said softly, "I'm sorry, kiddo. For real. But I can't talk to you." And he hung up.

At the Elkan Properties office, a recorded message told me a company spokesperson would make a statement at four. The phone clicked off automatically.

I called the young man who was doing the financial research and told him to get his sorry ass moving. I wanted results by the end of the day.

I called every contact I had or ever did have within the Police Department, but I got from all of them the same answer I had from Peter. Most of them were not nearly as polite.

I knew I would be at the Elkan offices at four for the announcement, but I thought I had enough time to go down to the building site first. I just wanted to look around. I didn't expect any work to be going on, but maybe Vera would be there. Maybe someone else who knew Alan. I wanted to talk to someone who knew him.

It was eerily quiet. I had never been there in daylight when there wasn't noise and bustle. Today everything was still, as silent as a cemetery.

I walked all around the outside, looking for any signs of life, but there were none until I returned to the front gate. Jerry Murtaugh was letting himself out.

His face was ashen. When I approached him, he growled, "Not today." I smelled beer on his breath. When I tried to say something, he glared at me. Then his expression changed. He must have seen something in my face, because his tone was suddenly softer when he said, "Hey, what's wrong with you?"

Unnerved by this unexpected gentleness, I could only shake my head.

"Was there somethin' between the two of you?" I nodded. "I thought so. I've known him a long time. I thought I saw the signs. Come on, I'll buy you a beer."

He led me to a tiny dark bar, empty in midafternoon. We sat at a back booth.

"I can't even take it in," he said. "Can't get it into my mind, you know, that he's gone. Let alone how it happened." He shook his head. "Just can't take it in. I knew him a long time. Even knew his family."

"How is his father—" I stopped. "I mean, how is he taking it? And his mother?"

"Mother's dead a long time. This'll probably kill the old man. He's a real sick man already, and Alan is his only kid. Was his only kid."

He looked at me and said, "I know you're a reporter. Are you here personal or professional?"

I tried to smile, but I could feel it wobbling. "Right now, it's personal. I'm—I guess I'm having trouble taking it in too."

"So, how involved were you?"

"Not very. Not really. But I liked him. I just liked him."

Murtaugh nodded. "Very likable guy. Always was. He was so excited about this building. Like a kid. You know? Bet he talked your ear off about it."

"Not really. I was writing a story about it, about

Vera's finds, really, but I was learning a lot about the building along the way, Alan's family and all. It made it hard to be involved with Alan at the same time.''

"I could see that it might." He looked at me appraisingly and asked again, "You sure this is personal? Strictly off the record?"

"Yes," I promised, "for now."

"Your friend Vera is being questioned by the police. Maybe even right now."

"That's ridiculous."

"No, it isn't. They picked her up from the site. I saw them."

I was so angry I couldn't even speak.

"Dr. Miss Vera was pretty vocal after the fire. Had a lot to say about Alan being responsible and how she'd get even."

"You heard her?" My stomach was tying itself into knots.

"Me, and everybody in ten blocks. She wasn't trying to keep it a secret."

"And you told the police?"

He shook his head. "Anyone could've told them. Probably heard it more than once."

"That's the stupidest thing I've ever heard."

"Police don't think so." He put his beer mug down, wiped his mouth, and said, "I have to be moving along. There's a coupla things I need to do, and I'm supposed to show up at that announcement later. Will I be seeing you there?"

"Yes, of course. Thanks for the beer."

"My pleasure," he said with a faint smile. "Thanks for the company."

I wasn't sorry to see him go. I needed to think, and think hard. I needed to ask a question, and I needed time to figure out how to get an answer. Finally I went to the pay phone and called Peter again.

As soon as he heard my voice, he said, "I meant it, Kay. I can't talk about it. Not at all. I shouldn't even be on the phone with you to say hello."

"Peter, listen, I did you a favor once, a long time ago." I said it fast so he wouldn't hang up.

"Yeah?"

"Think back. I found out something, and you begged me to sit on it for a day. Remember?"

He made a sound that might have been yes.

"I did it, and I never called in the favor, did I?"

He sounded grim when he said, "You saying this is payback time?"

"One question. That's all I want answered."

"I'm not promising. You'll have to run it by me."

"Was Alan Elkan shot with a .38?"

The sharp gasp gave me the answer, one I was hoping not to get, but he only said, "You know I can't tell you that."

"Then you still owe me one. Where is my friend Vera Contas right now?"

"On her way home. And you never talked to me today." The phone clicked off.

My knees sagged. I wiped my sweaty palms on my pants. My friend, my old friend Vera, owned a gun. One of her old Marlboro Men boyfriends had given it to her years and years ago, and insisted she learn how to use it too. A long-ago memory came back to me: Vera and me out in the country somewhere, in a field, and Vera showing me the gift from Bobby or Jimmy or whoever the hell it was.

I hadn't been too impressed. I'd already seen gunshot victims on city streets, and I'd grown up in rural America, where hunting guns were common and so were stupid and tragic gun accidents. I told her she was a damned fool.

She responded by suddenly lifting her arm, pointing the gun, and firing four bullets, hitting the same tree branch every time. She said, "You don't understand. Bobby's a real southern guy. He *likes* guns. He's also protective. He says anyone, male or female, who works out in deserted country places like I do needs protection. Isn't that sweet? He got it for me, and made me learn how to use it the right way."

The gun was a .38. I was sure I remembered that. I wondered whatever became of it. Did she still have it? Or had it disappeared during her wandering life? She was in some trouble, but not arrested, it seemed. She'd certainly be in more if the police knew about the gun. I wasn't even considering that Murtaugh's implications could be true. It was unthinkable, and I wouldn't think it. I wouldn't. My main concern at that moment was to reach Vera. I left her a message, said I'd call back, told her to call my office and leave messages, told her I knew what was going on, told her not to do anything rash. I put the phone down and wished I had a beeper.

I very much wanted to hear from Vera's own mouth that the gun had fallen to the bottom of the Mississippi, gone into the sacred well of the Mayas, was lost years ago in the Appalachian forest. That it wasn't anywhere near Alan's office and never had been.

I tried out in my mind a picture of Vera knocking on Alan's office door late at night, the gun concealed in her purse. He answers. She whips out the gun.... The picture ran in black and white in my mind, and I stopped it right there. I was imagining a scene in a bad film noir. The Barbara Stanwyck part just didn't fit Vera. Of course, it didn't fit quite a number of scary and very guilty other people I had seen over the years, either.

It was some time before the extremely odd fact hit me that my first interest was to see Alan's murderer brought to justice, and my second instinct was to help my friend. Maybe even those two were in conflict, but in a situation in which the story should have been number one, it was barely number three. That's when I knew for sure that somehow I had stopped being a reporter. I would have to deal with it later.

The press conference at Alan's office told me nothing. A company official spoke, not someone I'd ever seen before, and Jerry Murtaugh was there, looking pale and red-eyed. I wondered if he still smelled like a man who'd been drinking all morning.

We were told only that they were all shattered by Alan's death; that work would resume tomorrow as he would have wished, so that the completed building would be his monument; and that funeral plans were on hold, pending release of his body from the medical examiner's office.

In response to a question, the official said, "Our only word from the police is that they are pursuing leads and have nothing official to say at this time."

I expected nothing more, but I was somehow disappointed anyway. It was so bland and uninformative, it might as well have been a press conference at City Hall. I knew I was being ridiculous. Did I expect the grieving family to cry "Revenge!" as if it were a mob funeral? Or the murderer to lurk somewhere, unable to resist hearing his own publicity? I told myself to cut it out and get back to work.

At the office I found a message from the financial researcher. He wasn't done, but he'd be in touch the minute his report was ready.

Then Vera's tense voice came on. "I'm home, Kay. Got your message. I don't even know what's going on; how can you? But I'm glad you called. I'll be home. Call me," she stammered. "Just call."

Then I was shocked to hear Tony's voice, clear as could be from halfway around the world. "It's four a.m. here, and I can't sleep. I miss you more than words can describe. We finished our business today, and we're flying out tomorrow, but I have to take the girls back to their mother's in Detroit before I get home. Should I schedule myself through New York and be there next weekend? Leave me a message at my hotel in Detroit, the Grosse Pointe Hilton, 555-4197. If I were less lonely and exhausted, I probably wouldn't even admit this, but there hasn't been a minute since my last visit that you aren't with me, in some corner of my mind. I dunno. I hope I haven't just made a complete fool of myself. Goodnight."

It took my breath away. I wasn't sure I even deserved to be hearing that, since I couldn't honestly say the same. Yet somehow hearing those words, and in his voice, brought me out of the fog I'd been in all day. I immediately called his hotel and left a one-word message: "Yes." My hand, almost without my will, circled next weekend in red on my calendar. I stopped short, but only just, before adding stars.

I called Vera and told her not to move, I was on the way. I picked up a substantial order of Szechuan food and a quart of Rocky Road ice cream.

I considered Scotch, too, but rejected it. We needed well-fueled, but clear, heads tonight.

Vera looked awful, white-faced with purple shadows under her eyes.

"They asked me questions," she said indignantly, as soon as she opened the door. "The police. They questioned me for hours. Have you ever been in a police station? It is disgusting."

The enticing odors from my bag penetrated her distress and she said, "I couldn't eat a thing. I'm way too upset."

"Yeah, yeah," I said. "I can, anyway. Get bowls. And yes, I've been in a police station once or twice. Have you forgotten: Brenda Starr, Reporter?"

That got a faint smile. I put all the food out on her coffee table, and she dug in, apparently unaware of it as she continued her tirade.

"Kay, I got the feeling they think I might have killed Alan. *Me*. It was the most humiliating, most ridiculous. Me, of all people."

"If they don't know you have a gun already, they may find out anytime," I said flatly. "He was killed with a .38. Whatever happened to that gun you used to have?"

"Oh, my God," she said, understanding finally dawning. "They might really think I did it."

"Yes, *you,* you idiot, the person who threatened to get even in front of a cast of thousands."

"I didn't mean anything like that," she snapped. "I don't even know what I meant, I was so angry. I would have embarrassed him somehow, sued him, there are lots of ways to get even that aren't violent. Have you *ever* seen me do something violent?"

I had to say it. I looked her straight in the eyes and said, "Did you do it?" She slapped me.

I don't know which of us was more shocked. She turned red, then white, then stammered, "I didn't mean it. I don't even know what I'm doing."

"So much for nonviolence."

"Kay, I can't even kill mice in my apartment! You've seen me carry them outside in a jar. A person? Someone I knew? Knew fairly well?" She shuddered. "I didn't do it. I couldn't possibly have done it. I hated Alan for what he was doing to my work, but I didn't kill him. You can't believe anything else!"

I didn't know what I believed. I didn't think she was that good an actress, but I also thought that I didn't know her as well as I used to. I could only stick to facts. "Whatever became of that gun?"

"I took it to the site one day, when I began to

feel really threatened. I put it in the file cabinet under my desk, under a pile of papers, and just left it. I haven't even looked for it in a while."

"Dear Lord."

"Am I in a lot of trouble?"

"Maybe. Was it licensed?"

She shook her head. "I never bothered."

"Then you could be in trouble just for that. Vera, this isn't the backwoods. You should have more sense!" She nodded, not looking up at me. "Still, it probably means the police don't know about it yet. I mean, I assume if they had any real evidence you'd be arrested."

"They don't have any because there isn't any to have. Haven't you been listening? *I didn't do it!*"

I went right on. "A gun is going to make them very persistent, if they find out about it, at least until they know it wasn't the same one. I don't know much about this, but I think you need a criminal lawyer. I know a few good ones. I brought names and phone numbers with me. Now listen, Vera," I said as sternly as possible, "you're probably in big trouble. Forget about work. You can't dig from jail! Forget about everything and call these lawyers. Do it tonight and leave messages. I'm serious. Get expert advice right away."

"I will, Kay. Will you help me figure out what to say to them?"

So I stayed and helped and then went home.

Alone in my own apartment, I had to face up at last to the questions I'd been shoving underground all day: Was I helping an old friend unfairly in trouble? Or was I advising the woman who had murdered a man I was involved with? Sort of involved with? Not quite involved with? Whatever it was, he was dead, and I couldn't entirely convince myself the police were making a huge mistake. I'd be looking at Vera too. And yet I'd known her a long time. In that moment before she slapped me, I was sure I saw only anger at my question in her face, not guilt.

FIFTEEN

THE NEXT DAY was Saturday. There was no point in going to the office; there was nothing I could do there. I tried all my contacts at the police department; no one would talk to me. I called Vera, who said she was talking to lawyers and would call later. The researcher had left me a message, saying he was working full steam and would call as soon as he had a report ready. Suddenly I had nothing to do. Until that moment, I hadn't known it was the moment I had been dreading for the last twenty-four hours. As long as I'd been operating in overdrive, I didn't have to think. I didn't have to feel. Now there was nothing to do but think and feel.

I could think about Vera and whether she had a role in Alan's death. In the clear light of morning, I was no longer sure of what I had seen in Vera's face. I was slowly realizing that she had never expressed any dismay over Alan's death, let alone grief. Not surprising, given how she felt about him. But she had never expressed surprise or shock or even that most standard New Yorker's response, outrage at the crime. No, I was not at all sure about Vera this morning.

I could think about Alan and everything I didn't

know about him. Maybe that researcher would answer some of those questions. Or I could think about Alan and how I felt about him, or how I might have felt about him in a future that no longer existed.

I could think about myself and Alan and Tony. Had my nascent interest in Alan developed just because Tony was so far away? Or was he just another in my long line of what Vera dismissively called my ''lounge lizards,'' sophisticated men I'd managed to attract because I have a great diguise? I'm always surprised and grateful that they don't see through me to the small-town misfit I really am.

Tony was something else, a man from my long-ago past. Twenty years later we'd connected again, instantly. We seemed to know each other deeply, past and present. Maybe that was the trouble. Maybe I didn't want someone who knew me when. Maybe I only wanted a man who believed in my disguise.

I took a deep breath and forced myself to come to a complete stop. I jumped up to rummage around in my purse. My own car still sat there in the shop waiting for the insurance adjuster, but deep in my purse somewhere I would find the keys to the car Alan had loaned me. I'd never touched it, and I had no idea what to do with it now, but I saw no reason not to use it today. If I got in the car and drove fast enough, maybe I could outrun the questions.

Without really planning it, I found myself on the expressway, pointed toward Brighton Beach. It was a bright summer day, breezy, with blue skies. I played rock and roll loudly on the terrific radio and let the beat of the music and the salty wind from the harbor fill my head. Once I was past the endless construction around the Prospect Expressway, I flew along, admiring the way the view outside my window suddenly opened up to the wide mouth of the harbor, the sparkling expanse of water and sky, and the soaring arc of the Verrazano-Narrows Bridge. There were ships moving majestically through the Narrows and out to sea, and sailboats skimming back and forth like dragonflies. I stopped at a narrow strip of waterside park to admire the brilliantly colored kites soaring straight up to the clouds on the brisk breeze off the harbor, but the sight didn't lift my heart as it usually did.

I had my mother's address in my pocket. It was somewhere out here; the little street was lost in the folds of the map. It wasn't hard to find someone who could direct me. The second person I asked said in the accents of true Brooklyn, "Oh, yeah, it's over there. See the towers? It's one of those buildings." He turned to his companion. "Am I right? Is that an Elkan Towers address, or am I right?"

He turned back to me. "Ask anyone around there. They'll point ya to the right building."

So it turned out I'd already been there, where my mother lived. In the heat of August, a little chill ran down my back.

By now I knew how to go directly to the Towers, but I didn't go that way. I wasn't ready. I wandered in and out of Brighton Beach Avenue's exotic stores. I focused tightly on whether to buy and take home a selection of Russian pierogi, little packets of dough stuffed with a choice of fillings—spinach, meat, potato, cheese. I didn't even know how to cook them. I examined varieties of smoked fish, salmon, sturgeon, sable, knowing quite well that I couldn't carry them with me for hours on this hot day. I considered a king's ransom worth of caviar.

I lingered in the Black Sea Book Shop, where there wasn't a book or magazine not printed in the Cyrillic alphabet, which I could not read, and wondered if I'd like a tape of Russian popular songs that I would not understand. I left, and contemplated a lunch counter offering fried chicken, pizza, and Russian pelmeni, and a restaurant listing sushi and pierogi.

When I finally ran out of ways to stall, I walked over to the Towers. Following the winding paths inside the development, trying to make sense of the confusing numbering system on the identical buildings, I found the right one by accident. Just inside the outer door there was a row of buttons next to a list of names and apartment numbers. Could I just ring her bell, and when she asked on the intercom, "Who's there?" say, "Your daughter"?

I stood there, looking at the names, for a long time. When I finally left, I sat on a bench opposite the entrance, watching the women go in and out, the ones in their late fifties. She was only seventeen when I was born. The Cousin Sally of my childhood was just a dim fragment of a memory, a laughing voice and red hair. I didn't see anyone today I could match with that. I couldn't even remember her face. Could she be one of the fit, youthful-looking, gray-haired women I saw jogging? Could she be the brassy blond coming up the walk, in a sequined T-shirt and a bitter expression? The proudly smiling grandmother, deftly maneuvering a huge baby carriage into the building? Funny. Until that moment, I had never thought of the possibility that she'd had other children. Sitting there suddenly became unbearable. I walked away swiftly, but with no real purpose, and I ended up at the beach.

On a hot Saturday in August, the beach was carpeted with nearly naked, well-oiled bodies. I had to stick to the boardwalk to be able to walk at all. I would not think about my mother anymore right now. I made a firm decision about that, and repeated it to myself several times. In the midst of radios blasting rock and rap and salsa, the smell of hot greasy french fries and spicy franks sizzling on grills, the small plane overhead trailing an advertising banner for a rockin' radio station, and under-lying it all, the faint sound of the waves and the gulls crying, I willed myself to set it all aside and think about Alan. I concentrated so hard I could have been on a gray, deserted November beach.

In my mind, I arranged everything I knew on file cards, one fact to a card, and shuffled them again and again until a pattern started to appear. When it did, I wondered why it had taken me so long.

I left the boardwalk and turned toward Anatoly Sorkin's gym. Would he be there on a Saturday? I rang the doorbell, and he came hurrying to answer it, his expression surprised and wary until he saw me.

"Miss Kay! This is happy surprise. I wondered what nuisance could be disturbing my work time, but you it is good to see." He looked at me more carefully and said, "But what is trouble I see in your face? Come in and tell me. I make tea; we talk."

The glass of hot, sweet tea was strangely refresh-ing, and as we sipped, I tried to tell him.

"Yes," he said soberly. "Is very tragic, a young man losing his life, and in such a way. All this neighborhood talks of it, you know, because family is so well known here."

"And what do they say, all the neighborhood?"

He shrugged. "Everyone has different theory. Is

drug addicts. Is robbery. Is woman scorned. They know nothing."

There was something odd in his open face, something furtive and reluctant.

"Are there people who do know something?" He still hesitated. "Anatoly, he was my friend. Someone I cared about. Please tell me if there's more."

"Is just gossip, you know."

"I understand."

"Some people say it is no robbery at all. News says there was no break-in, no robbery. Some people believe it has to do with father, old business, ugly business at bottom."

And that was one of the ways the index cards had arranged themselves in my mind. Always excepting the possibility that it really was Vera after all.

"Who says that? Who knows about it? Do you?"

"No, not me. I hear stories, but this was before my time in America. I have friend who knows, maybe. He knows everything about neighborhood."

"Yes?"

"Sometimes they call him 'Mayor of Brighton Beach.' He always live here, he knows everyone, he is in every organization. It is his life work, you understand, to keep Brighton Beach great place to live."

My face must have lit up, because he offered before I even asked. "I call him now. Wait here."

He disappeared into his office, and I was alone with my scattered thoughts and half-formed theories. One moment it all made sense; the next I thought it was like a cat's cradle. Pull too hard on one strand, and it would all come apart.

Anatoly returned, grinning. "You want to meet old man Elkan? Now, this afternoon?"

"What?"

"He is here, in neighborhood. My friend will take you. Come, we meet my friend right now."

His friend was an old man, very bald, with a white mustache and shrewd old eyes. He insisted that I call him Maxie, and suggested we talk while we walk.

"I'm living in Brighton Beach eighty years. Did young Anatoly tell you that? I've seen plenty of changes over the years, plenty of changes, but it's still the finest neighborhood in Brooklyn. No, you just can't beat it.

"Now, you want to hear about the Elkans? Me and Stan go way back. Come up as boys here, Stan and me, going to school, getting in trouble, but we didn't do so bad for ourselves, either one of us. Course, Stan made a lot more money than me, but it was his wife wanted to move out of the neighborhood and up in the world, she thought it was. But Stan, he always kept his roots here. Kept his main office right here. That's where we're going now."

"Is he there now? Today? I'm very surprised. I mean, with his son—"

"Well, see, this is where Stan's friends are. Stan don't have much family, and what he has, he don't like. Wife's gone. No other kids. So he's here, and here's where people come to see him. Funeral's held up because of the murder, you know. Stan doesn't even have the body yet, so they can't do normal mourning, but it's good for him to be someplace where friends can come pay respects."

He gave me a sharp look. "How do you want me to introduce you?"

"Just say I'm a friend of Alan's."

He glanced from Anatoly to me and back. "That's the truth? I thought Anatoly said you're a reporter."

"Yes, I am," I admitted. "But Alan was a friend. I hadn't known him long. We were just getting to know each other, really, but I liked him, and I feel so—cheated." As the words came out, I recognized it for the truth.

"We all do," he said quietly, patting my hand. "We all do. So, I'll just say 'friend' and leave out the reporter part. Stan don't like reporters, and he has good reasons."

"It makes me feel kind of paranoid. I don't know why everyone dislikes us so much," I said, not very honestly. I gave him my best innocent look. "I just try to do my job, but everyone thinks I'm out for blood."

"I'm sure you're not," he said, patting my hand again, "but plenty of them are. Stan had a little business, let's say"—he paused—"a little business difficulty, and those reporters blew it way up, way out of proportion. You know, anything for a headline."

I remembered the *Daily News* headlines and nodded. "What was the truth, then, if the reporters didn't get it right?" Here was someone with a personal knowledge of the story. What luck.

"They got nothin' right. Oh, okay, a coupla things." He ticked them off on his fingers. "One, Stan put up the Towers. Two, they were partly government funded. Three, he borrowed money like any businessman. But all that stuff about his investors being crooks, the mob, all that crap, you should excuse my language. Old friends from the neighborhood, that's all. And for all the smoke, they never found a fire. Never."

Behind him, Anatoly looked at me and shook his head, his expression one of great skepticism, but he put a finger to his lips.

"Well, here we are." Maxie Fiedler stopped in front of a modest storefront office in a two-story brick building. The sign said only, "S. Elkan, Inc., Real Estate."

"Young Anatoly here couldn't get you in," Maxie said with a smug grin, "because he don't really know Stan, but I can." He rang the bell, and the door was opened by a man who seemed to fill the entire doorway. He wore a dark suit and a scowl, but my guide was not impressed.

"Tell Stan it's Maxie, come to call with a friend who wants to pay respects."

The man turned, and I was sure the loose fit of his jacket concealed a gun. I'd been around enough cops to recognize that particular cut of jacket. He was surprisingly heavy muscle to be the doorman for an ordinary business.

SIXTEEN

THE MUSCLE CAME BACK with a fractionally more cordial expression and led us to an office in the back. It was full of sober-faced people in dark clothes, talking quietly to each other, but the center of the subdued activity was an old man sitting on a small sofa. He was tiny, shrunken, and his drawn face was the faint yellow of old ivory. I could believe that he was a sick man. Alan's father. I wondered for a mini-second if my mother looked this old; then I forced myself back into the present moment.

"Stan?" Maxie said it softly.

The old man opened his eyes and said wearily, "Ah, Maxie, my friend. Good of you to come. I knew you would."

"Stan, I was here this morning."

The old man looked confused, then said quietly, "I meant 'again,' Max. I knew you would come *again*. And who is this?"

"Anatoly, you have met before. He walked over with us. This is Kay Engels, who was a friend of Alan's."

I bent over to shake his hand, and then stood up just as someone came into the room behind him. I found myself staring right into the surprised face of Jerry Murtaugh. He didn't appear happy to see me, and didn't say hello, but I could feel his eyes on me throughout my entire conversation with Stanley Elkan.

I had to search for the right words, both the ones from my heart and the ones that would get me what I wanted from him.

"Mr. Elkan, this is an honor. Alan used to talk about you a lot."

"Did he?" His face brightened. "My son talked about me with you? We had our differences over the years, you know. Many of them." His face crumpled. "Now there are no more years to make it up."

"I know he wanted to," I said quickly. Maybe it wasn't even untruthful. He never said he didn't want to. I went on, "He was a good person, thoughtful and kind. And ambitious. He was so excited about his project."

"Project?" The old man looked confused. "We're not building a housing project here for low-life trash. This is a *development*. Big difference, you know. First-class apartments for middle-class tenants. And they'll name it after me: Elkan Towers."

The men around him grew silent, and Murtaugh whispered in his ear. He listened, blinked, and turned to me with a gracious smile.

"Of course, that was long ago. That was *my* big success. Alan has his own dreams. He wants to build a big Manhattan building."

"I know," I said confidingly. "I know. He told me all about it."

He gave me a considering look. "Who are you? How did you know my son?"

"I'm Kay Engels, Mr. Elkan. A mutual friend introduced me to Alan. We had dinner a few times. I'm going to miss him."

"Pretty girl like you," he said pleasantly. "Alan should have brought you to visit me."

"He would have," I said reassuringly. "He would have, but he was so busy. And he seemed worried too. Something about his business worried him, but he wouldn't tell me. Did he ever tell you what it was?"

"Alan worried? No." He sighed. "He never told me much. Didn't think I knew anything. Didn't think I would understand. Maybe not, but I helped him with the money, got my friends to buy in. Never thanked me."

He closed his eyes, and I couldn't tell if he was dismissing me or if he'd drifted into sleep. Either way, it seemed he wasn't going to talk any more to me. Maxie gently touched my arm and led me away. There were other people waiting to pay respects.

In a corner of the room, out of the crowd, he

whispered, "Poor old Stan. He's losing it, ya know. Sometimes he's right there, running the show like always; then other times he's like today, drifting in and out. Course, with the shock and all, it's only to be expected, I guess. Makes me feel like maybe I'm getting old, seeing him like that."

We left, and were only a few steps up the street when Jerry Murtaugh caught up with us. He had two very large men in suits with him. One was the surly doorkeeper we had met earlier. Murtaugh took my arm in a bruising grip and said to my companions, "We'd like a private word with Miss Engels. She'll catch up with you."

Anatoly seemed to shift his weight, taking a firmer stance, and stared straight at him, but his voice was quiet. He said only, "We are out for a walk together. We wait with her, I think."

Murtaugh shrugged, still holding my arm, and said, "Have it your way, but walk over there with my friends. My conversation with Miss Engels here is private." He turned me to face him, grasped both arms, and said, "What are you doing here?"

"I think you heard Mr. Fiedler introduce me. I wanted to pay respects to Mr. Elkan."

He gave me a hard stare and said, "Naah. If that was all, you could have waited for the memorial service. I don't think you were that close to Alan; I've done some asking around. You went to some trouble to track Stan down on this private day, and

I want to know why. Seems like you were trying to ask him questions. It looked a lot like prying to me."

I didn't say a word. I just stared straight back at him and left a silence for him to fill.

"I think you're here as a reporter, not as Alan's friend." His hands tightened. "Leave the Elkans alone. Hear me? Stan's old and sick, and he's got nothin' to tell you. He wouldn't even have let you in if he'd have known who you really were. And he's got a lot of friends to protect his son's memory."

He glanced at the two other men, who stood behind my friends. Only I could see as they let their jackets slide open to reveal the guns in their shoulder holsters. He tightened his grip on my arms even more. I could feel the bruises forming. Then he let me go so suddenly I almost fell. He turned toward the Elkan office, only looking back to say to me, "Remember what I said."

My companions hurried to me, their faces full of concern. Maxie patted my hand and said, "Are you all right? We couldn't hear nothin'."

I said, shakily, "Yes. Sure. I'm fine." I forced myself to stop, reflexively rubbing the sore spots on my arms where Murtaugh had grabbed me. "I'm fine. He was just apologizing for Mr. Elkan's confusion and asked me not to spread it around."

Anatoly's face told me he didn't believe a word

of it, but Max nodded. "I know that guy," he said. "Know his face, anyway. He worked for Stan for years and years. Protective bunch of guys working for Stan, ya know. Lot of loyalty there."

Maxie left us after a few blocks, with a cheery invitation to look him up anytime. As soon as he was gone, Anatoly turned to me and said, "Now tell me what really happened. No more fairy tales."

"How did you know?"

"You think these thugs are different from Russian secret police? Ha! I know what they are. One look, and I know."

When I was done telling, he said, "Miss Kay, I am sorry I helped you today, because maybe it not such a help. These are dangerous men."

"They want us to think so."

"No, no, no! Look, I hear stories. Bad men work for Elkan. Bad things happen to people they don't like. If they tell you to stay away, they mean it."

"They're punks. I have a dead friend, and another friend suspected of killing him, and dammit, I hate cover-ups. All right," I said, as much to myself as to him, "maybe I've had enough of reporting. Maybe I'm tired and want out, but I've been a reporter all my adult life. If someone tries to scare me off, I know that's where the story is."

"Miss Kay, Miss Kay," Anatoly whispered, "you are too excited for a public place." I was so angry, I'd forgotten we were walking on the street.

"Now shush, and listen to me. You must not come back here asking questions. You must not. If they see you are ignoring them, it will be very bad." He looked at me. "Okay, okay, I see stubborn face like mule. If you come, call me first. I go with you, wherever you go, or another friend of mine goes. Is not safe otherwise. You promise?"

"No, I don't promise! Anatoly, this is sweet, but I don't need a bodyguard, and certainly not on crowded streets in Brooklyn in broad daylight."

"No? So, okay, so maybe you think you know what you're doing. Does not mean you do. Please. I like to see you again. I like to invite you to anniversary party in February. Like to have you write story when I have first national champion. This will not happen if you get hurt."

"I'll be careful, Anatoly, I'll promise that much. I am an adult woman, you know, and I've been doing this a long time."

He shrugged. "Call me anyway. Now, how you go home? Train?"

"I drove."

"Where is car? I walk you there."

Over my protests, he did just that, and waited until I had pulled away from the curb and was on my way to the expressway.

When I got home I found some reason to think Anatoly might have been right about the danger. My apartment had been ransacked. In the first moment of shock, I didn't know if the mess or the sense of invasion was more upsetting. Desk and dresser drawers had been pulled out, and the contents were strewn all over the floor; sofa cushions were scattered on the floor, too; my bed was stripped, the bedclothes tossed on the floor; but, I saw quickly, the stereo and television were still there. My few silver pieces had been knocked around but not removed. After a dreary couple of hours setting everything to rights, it was clear to me that the only thing missing was my file on the Elkan story.

It was not the disaster they had undoubtedly intended. Everything in the file was stored on my computer's hard drive. And I kept a backup copy at the office. I had been more concerned about a power failure than burglars, but I blessed the computer tech who'd browbeaten me into always backing up everything. I powered on, hit a few keys, and facts about the Elkans sprang up on my screen. Either they hadn't had time to trash the computer records, or they hadn't thought of it. Or they didn't know how.

Still, it was obvious they thought they had done some damage. I couldn't have overlooked the theft of the file. It had been in plain sight, plainly labeled. Were they trying to hide it by making it look like a burglary? Or were they just having fun, making a mess, and they intended me to know they had been there, and for a reason? That it wasn't a robbery?

I realized too late that I shouldn't have touched anything until I'd called the police. I'd have to report the break-in anyway, and I wasn't bringing it to my local precinct. I'd take it straight to the team working on Alan's murder. It was certainly connected somehow.

As I explained, the voice on the other end of the phone went with almost comical speed from bored to alert to "I'll handle it right away, ma'am. I'll phone it in myself, and you'll be contacted very shortly."

Just after I hung up, Vera called, saying in one long breath, "I can't tell you where I am. I hired one of your lawyers, and she said I should lay low for a few days, go to a hotel, make it hard for the police to find me, just long enough for us to make some plans."

"Vera—"

"No one is supposed to know where I am. Just wanted to let you know I'm all right. I'll call you."

Before I could say another word, she was gone, and I was left standing there with the phone in my hand, all my questions unanswered.

I finally had a chance to stretch out on my sofa, kick the shoes off my tired feet, and try to gather my scattered thoughts. Then the downstairs doorbell rang. I could see police officers on the stoop outside, so I buzzed them in and waited at my open apartment door. There were two of them in uniform, and two in plainclothes, my friend Peter one of them. He didn't look like a friend at that moment. He looked like a tough, determined, professional cop.

"You guys are terrific," I said. "I only called a few minutes ago, and here you are."

"You called? That's not why we're here."

"It isn't? I had a break-in here today. They made a big mess, but the only thing they took was my file on the Alan Elkan story. I called the special number for information on it."

"Yeah? They didn't get it to us yet. We can take a report while we're here, but"—he looked around—"this doesn't look like a break-in."

"I cleaned up. I just wasn't thinking. Guess I should have left it for some of you to see."

"I'd say so," Peter said with some sarcasm. "I'd expect you to know better. How do we even know a break-in took place now?"

I hadn't expected a hostile response from him. "Why would I lie about it?"

"Don't know if you would. Don't know if you wouldn't, either. How about a truthful answer to this? Is Vera Contas here?"

"No."

"Where is she?"

"I don't know," I said with complete honesty.

"She's not at home?" I asked, less honestly. I wanted to know what was going on here.

"Nope. She was seen leaving with a suitcase a couple of hours ago. We know you're friends, so we thought she might've come here, or you'd know where she went."

"I don't, and I'm not sure I'd have to tell you if I did know."

"There might be a difference of opinion on that. We have a warrant for her arrest."

I hid my gasp by swallowing hard. "Peter, please tell me what's going on."

"First tell me where she is."

"The hell I will! She called and told me she was disappearing for a while. She didn't even give me a chance to ask where."

"In the city? Out of town?"

"I don't even know that!" Was I screaming, or did it just feel that way? I forced my voice back to calm. "Look, Peter, I really don't know anything at all. And if I do find out, why should I tell you? You haven't shown me that warrant, and you haven't told me a thing. You're asking me to believe that a friend of almost twenty years killed another friend. That's ridiculous!"

The tough-cop attitude softened just a little. "I know she's your friend, Kay. That's why we're here. But you've got to believe we've got reasons to be looking for her. If you know anything, it's important that you tell us."

"Come on, Peter. 'Got to believe' doesn't make it with me. You know better."

"All right, all right." He seemed to be making a decision. "Kay, she owned a gun. We found it, and leaned on ballistics hard."

I was determined that my face wouldn't give anything away. If he said what I was afraid to hear, he would never know how much it felt like a punch in the stomach. I folded my hands together so he couldn't see them shaking.

"They matched, Kay. Her gun killed Elkan. Now do you believe us?" He gave me a suddenly suspicious look. "And why did you ask me what kind of gun was used, the other day? Did you know she had a gun?"

Somehow I made my lips move and my voice work. I ignored his question by asking my own.

"How did you find out about the gun?"

"Someone saw it in her desk, in that shed she uses. What's his name? Worked for Elkan?"

"Murtaugh?" One of the cops supplied the name.

"Yeah, that's him. Told us he'd seen it there in the drawer after all the trouble started. Thought we'd want to know."

"I'll just bet he did. That's all you've got?"

"All? You know damn well it's not chopped liver. It's a lot."

"Where did you find it? The gun?"

"Right in the drawer where he said it was."

"And you think she murdered someone and put the weapon away just like that, where other people had seen it? Peter, she's not stupid! Why would she do that?"

"Don't know, Kay. That's just one of the things we'd like to ask her. Which is why we'd like your help if you hear from her." He paused, then added, "If you do hear from her, and *don't* tell us, we could make it a big problem for you. Show her the warrant, Ritchie, just so she knows I'm telling the truth."

Phrases like "obstructing justice" and "harboring a fugitive" were swimming around in my mind.

"There's nothing I can tell you, Peter, about Vera." That much, at least, I could say firmly. "There *is* something I should tell you about Jerry Murtaugh, though."

I related my Brighton Beach encounter with Murtaugh, and told him the details about my apartment break-in.

He listened, and one of the other cops took notes. "We'll have someone look into the break-in, Kay."

"And Murtaugh?"

"Yeah, we'll look into him too, but we still want

Vera Contas." His last words to me were "Remember what I said."

It was the second time in two days someone had told me that. Were they warnings or threats? I just about didn't care. I was tired of being pushed around, and I was angry.

I was angry at Vera, too, angry at her for keeping a gun, angry at her for involving me, angry at her for being so all-around stupid. Especially angry at her for making me wonder if the cops weren't right about her.

SEVENTEEN

WHEN THE PHONE RANG, I snapped, "Yes?"

A soft, startled male voice at the other end stammered, "Miss Engels?"

"Yes," I snapped again. "Who is this?"

"This is Mike McIntyre. From Noll Associates?" It was the financial researcher. "You seemed anxious for my report, so I was checking to see if you got my fax?"

"You sent a fax?" That got my attention.

"Yes, about four o'clock. The machine reported it was a completed transmission, but I wondered if you had any questions."

"Mike, please hold for a minute." I checked the table where my fax machine sits. I checked the floor around it. I checked the wastebasket where I'd thrown away papers when I had cleaned up the mess.

"Mike, there's no fax here. This is important. Tell me exactly when you sent it and where." I was aware I was still snapping, but I didn't care at that moment. I could apologize later.

"I have the printout right here. Four-oh-seven, to 555-8331. But can't you print something that tells you what your machine received?"

"Ouch. I forgot about that. I probably can. I just got the machine, and I haven't figured it all out. Can you possibly send it again?"

"No problem, and I'll be here this evening if you want to call me. My phone number is on the cover sheet."

In the meantime, I thought glumly, I'd have to find the manual and figure out how to do a report. By the time his message was coming through, I had it figured out. Press 22. Press #1. Press Start. That's all it took.

He'd sent it, just as he'd said; my machine had received it; it wasn't here now. I wondered if the break-in artists who'd taken my file had found it. I wondered even more after I read the report.

Interviews with suppliers indicated ever-later payments of bills, and some had cut off credit entirely. There were liens on some of Alan's other properties. Interviews with other builders brought out the same rumors again and again: Every penny Alan had was in the new building. Stan Elkan's old friends had recently taken a substantial piece of Alan's business. He was having trouble getting tenants to commit because they weren't sure the building would be finished on time. Too many rumors, but the limited public documents seemed to support some of them.

I sat up late that night, drinking Scotch, reading the report, rewriting my notes, constructing and reconstructing the possibilities. I thought for a long time about sharing what I'd learned with the cops. I was still thinking about it when I drifted off to sleep on the sofa.

THE RINGING PHONE startled me out of a deep, hungover sleep. I reached for the phone with my eyes still closed, brain still snoozing. An unfamiliar voice politely said, "May I please speak to Miss Kay Engels?"

I groaned silently and thought, If it's someone selling a newspaper subscription, I'll tell them I'm not there. I opened one eye to check the clock. 11: 20 a.m. Okay. Not so early.

Through the fog in my brain I enunciated carefully, "This is she."

I heard someone take a deep breath. "Kay, I'm calling in response to your letter. It was thoughtful of you to write. This is Sally."

My brain snapped on, and my eyes snapped open. "Sally, can you hold for just a second? I'll be right back."

I ran to the kitchen, splashed cold water on my face, poured a cold Pepsi in lieu of the coffee I hadn't made, and picked up the phone again.

"Thank you for calling," I said. "I...it's...well, it's amazing to hear your voice after all these years."

"Do you remember me?" She sounded surprised.

"I do, just a little. You had red hair. I remember that."

"I still do. Of course, it's helped out a lot by Clairol now."

"And you laughed a lot. And you sent great presents. I remember a kaleidoscope."

"You remember that? I'm so glad. I went all the way to FAO Schwarz for it. I wanted the best one I could find."

"And a bracelet with a charm that was a tiny music box. And a book of fairy tales with the most wonderful illustrations. I don't know what happened to the other things, but I still have that one."

There was a long silence. When she spoke again, her voice shook. "It means so much to me that you remember those things." She stopped, then said more firmly, "I did know about your parents' deaths, all that long time ago. I had a nice visit with your mother, just before she passed on, but I know I should have written to you, or come to the funeral, but you see, there were all these reasons..."

She didn't know that I knew a lot about the reasons. I said quickly, "It doesn't matter. I'm just so glad that you called."

"Kay, would it be too much to ask—could we get together sometime? You asked in your letter if I'd like any of your parents' things for a keepsake, and I don't know about that, I don't remember what they had, but it would be such a pleasure just to sit and talk with you. I'd like to find out all about you. You are...you would be...your mother was..." A deep breath. "She was my cousin, of course. And seeing you would be like finding a piece of my youth again. If that doesn't sound silly."

No, I thought, it doesn't sound silly. It sounds like my own voice talking.

"I would like that," I said. My voice, made calm by sheer willpower, drowned out my beating heart. "When could we do that?"

"I'm not sure. I'd be happy to go into the city to see you, but I live as sort of a companion to an elderly man, and he hasn't been well lately. A neighbor could stay with him for a little while, but I can't leave for long. Maybe next week he'll be back to normal, and I can get away."

"I'm free today," I said. "Why wait? I could come to see you."

"You could? That would be wonderful. I see from your letter that you're on the Upper West Side. You know Brooklyn? Do you know where Brighton Beach is?"

I was glad she couldn't see my face. "I've been there," I said. "I could find my way. Where can we meet?"

"Not here where I live. There's a nice little place right near the subway stop on Brighton Beach Avenue. It's an elevated train; you take the rear stairs, and you can't miss it. It's called Beach Pastry. We can meet there, and if you don't like it, then we can always go someplace else."

"That sounds perfect. Is two o'clock good? I can't wait—"

"Nothing will keep me from it. You'll know me by my red hair and the biggest smile in the place."

"I'll see you then. I'm tall with black hair, and—" I glanced quickly at my closet "—I'll be in a flowered skirt and sandals."

"I'll know you," she said softly. "I would know you anywhere."

I whirled into action. Shower, coffee, breakfast. Clothes. What did I need to bring?

The phone rang. I cursed, and let the machine answer it. Nothing, but nothing, was going to side-track my plans for today. At the moment I really didn't care about Vera's situation, or my story, or the police.

It was Anatoly, so I did pick up as he was in mid-message.

"I am calling to see if you are taking my words yesterday seriously. You are not foolishly going back to Elkan's office?"

"Oh, no. No, I have other plans. Today I am going to see a long-lost relative."

"Is joke? Sounds ridiculous."

"Oh no, it's no joke. It's a real person, right out there in the real Brooklyn."

"Brooklyn? Kay, no games, please. What is this about Brooklyn? Where in Brooklyn?"

"Anatoly, what is this about questions? I'm not your child. I'm not your wife. I don't owe you any explanations! I am going to Brighton Beach today, but it has nothing to do with the Elkans. It's just a coincidence. It's strictly personal, and I don't have to discuss it with you."

"I did not mean to offend," he said stiffly. "I am worried about you, is all."

"Look, Anatoly," I relented. "I am meeting a relative at Beach Pastry, near the subway stop. You know it?"

"Yes."

"Okay. Is it public enough? Crowds of people in a busy street on Sunday? Nowhere near the Elkan office? I'm just going to have cake and coffee and a talk. Okay?"

"Do what you will," he said. "I think you should not come here, but if you will be stubborn, at least be careful." He hung up. I was sure he slammed the receiver down.

I didn't care. I drove out, and sang all the way. I parked a few blocks away and made my way along crowded Brighton Beach Avenue. Shoppers were out in force. The sun was shining. An officer was ticketing illegally parked cars. A police car was

patrolling the avenue. Anatoly was way too paranoid. I wondered idly if years in the Soviet Union
had done that to him. Nothing could happen here
today. The everyday quality of the street was itself
reassuring. And I was about to meet my mother.

As I crossed the street opposite the pastry shop,
I took a deep breath to control the flutters in my
stomach. I stepped into the street, preoccupied with
what I would say to her, and I looked up toward
the shop just in time to see a redheaded woman
scanning the street. That was the last thing I was
sure of. Everything after that happened in a blur.

A car pulled up in front of me, double-parking
and blocking my way across the street. I turned to
go around it just as the redhead across the street
seemed to focus on me. A man, a large man,
jumped out of the car, gripped my arm hard, and
said quietly, "Get in the car." He pushed me toward the open door.

"No! Get away!" I shouted. I think I looked
across the street again as I tried to pull my arm
away.

The iron grip tightened. Just as the car door
closed, and just before the man punched me in the
mouth, I managed to yell, "Sally!" I thought I saw
the woman's head snap around in my direction.

I was struggling in the backseat of the car, trying
to get free before the car began to move, but I
thought I caught a glimpse through the window of

a shadow detaching itself from the deeper shadows under the tracks. Was it Anatoly? Fighting with my captor, I couldn't see what was happening on the street.

After he hit me again, I couldn't struggle or even think for a few minutes. By the time my head stopped swimming, he was holding a gun on me, and the car was moving slowly through traffic. I lay quietly, letting him think he had knocked me out while I tried to assess the situation.

All right, I admitted to myself, I was scared. This was altogether too real and too personal. While I still didn't understand what was going on, I'd been a damn fool not to be taking it more seriously. What had happened to my street smarts? My reporter smarts? My plain common sense? Through the pain in my jaw I thought, Anatoly, my friend, you were right all along.

EIGHTEEN

I OPENED MY EYES just enough to begin to get my bearings. I was lying on the backseat of a car. It was dark inside, dark leather and dark-tinted windows. I stirred slightly, testing, and instantly felt cold metal pressed to my temple. Lying on the seat, I couldn't see my captor's face, only his thigh next to me. It looked big.

I stirred again and immediately heard a voice. "Don't try to get up. We want you right there." I felt the tip of the gun barrel again.

"Why?" I mumbled, face against the seat.

"You can't make trouble in that position, and no one can see you." It was a different voice, coming from the front seat.

"Why are you doing this? Where are we going?"

"Favor to a friend," the front-seat voice said. It was a familiar voice. "And you'll know where when we're ready to show you. Not before."

The ride felt endless. We seemed to be on city streets in stop-and-go traffic. Then there was a short, smooth stretch, as if we were on an expressway. More streets, then the car slowed as we drove over a bumpy, rutted road, either unpaved or in serious disrepair. I passed the time trying to figure out if I could possibly outrun two men with a gun, and decided I couldn't.

The car stopped. The man in front got out, and I heard a scraping sound. We moved forward a few yards, the scraping sound again, and the man returned. Did he open and close a gate?

We stopped, and I was dragged roughly out of the car. We were standing in a crumbling parking lot in front of a collection of derelict factories or warehouses. It was on the waterfront somewhere. I heard the faint slapping of water on piers or rocks and smelled that unmistakable mixture of salt water, fish, and fuel.

Now that I could see my captors, I recognized two of them as the thugs from Stan Elkan's office. The third one, in the front seat giving orders, was Jerry Murtaugh. He looked at me as if we'd never met or talked or had a beer together, and said, "Take her inside." He jerked his head toward one of the desolate buildings.

"No!" I locked my knees and pulled backward.

"You're not in a position to argue with us," he said with indifference. "You can walk in, we can drag you in, or we can just as easily shoot you right here and carry your body in."

"I'll walk." They held my arms painfully, as if to prevent me from getting away, but in any case, there was nowhere to run. We were surrounded by deserted-looking buildings. There was not another person, an open building, a public place, a phone, anywhere in sight. No doubt that was why they had chosen to bring me here.

The building we entered was dark and dank, but they led me upstairs into an office that seemed to be in use. There were working lights, a few couches and chairs, a small table. The men had a key to the place and found the light switches without effort. They'd been here before. They shoved me onto a couch and settled themselves on the seats, with a gun still pointed at me.

My mind was racing, but I saw no way out for now. There was only the one door we had just come through. When in trouble, stall, I thought. Ask questions.

"Why are we here?"

"Waiting for dark." I didn't like the sound of that.

"What then?"

At that, Murtaugh looked right at me. "You'd rather not know," he said, "and we'd rather not tell you."

"Yeah," the bigger of the two others chimed in. "Who needs a hysterical chick on our hands while we wait?"

"I could stop the hysterics easy," the other one said. "So could you." He was the smaller, meaner-looking one. He had a thin mouth and eyes that were way too glittering.

"Shut up," Murtaugh said without anger. "We'll do it the way we were told."

"Besides," the big guy said, "I got to go now and take a message. I'll come back later and tell you what they said to do with her."

Murtaugh said, "You've got your car?"

"Yeah, parked in back. You two can handle this?"

"Two of us, and I've got this?" The evil-looking one lifted the hand that held the gun. "And one skinny chick? Oh, sure, Jerry and I can just about manage to deal with it on our own, muscle man."

I thought they could too. Altogether too well. I can't panic, I told myself. If I do, I'm dead. Probably literally. If you don't, a little voice in my mind told me, you're probably dead anyway. No, I told myself, I can't think about that. So say something. Distract them. Ask more questions. Everyone likes to talk about themselves, if you ask the right questions. There are no exceptions. I have asked questions of much smarter people, and scarier ones, too—though not while they were pointing a gun at me. Act now.

I blurted out, "Are you the ones who broke into my apartment yesterday?"

The two remaining men looked at each other, and

then Murtaugh shrugged and said, "Why not? Makes no difference now."

"Yeah, it was us."

"Nice job," I said, trying to force admiration into my voice. "You just about fooled me into thinking it was an ordinary break-in, but you really only wanted my files on the Elkans, didn't you?"

"You figured that out?"

"You didn't take anything else. You left a TV, stereo, pictures—"

"Idiots," Murtaugh said without anger.

"Bet you didn't find the bug on your phone," the other one said.

"No, I didn't. That was neatly done. That's how you knew where to find me today, isn't it? And you found the fax my researcher sent, didn't you?"

He nodded.

"He sent me another one, you know. And I stored it at my office. Electronically. It's all sitting in my office computer right now, whatever happens to me. Think you can break into that skyscraper, one of the largest companies in America?"

"If we have to."

"You're bluffing." I looked away and half closed my eyes, as if bored with the entire conversation. The trick worked. He started to get angry.

"Should I show her who's bluffing?" I felt the gun in my ribs.

"Shut up," Murtaugh said calmly. "I want to

hear about this." He turned to me. "You saying everything in the file we took is on another computer?"

I nodded.

He thought a minute, then said, "It probably doesn't matter. I don't think anyone but us would know how close you were getting. And you were close enough to put it together any minute."

"What was I so close to? As you said, it doesn't matter if I know now. It would be nice to know why I—" I couldn't say it. "Why all this is happening."

He shrugged again. "Why not? We've got time. What do you already know?"

"Alan was behind schedule on the building," I said slowly, working it out. "He was carrying heavy bank loans, and the talk was that he had less official loans from unofficial sources too. Every day the building got behind, he was going deeper in debt just on the huge interest payments."

"Right so far. Can you guess the rest?"

"Those unofficial sources were getting worried?"

"Right again."

"And Vera's discovery might just cause the additional delays that would sink the whole project financially. The worried guys were, maybe, Stan Elkan's old associates, the ones who provided, maybe, dirty money for Stan's projects?" He nodded again. "Was their investment some kind of illegal loan? Or was it laundering?"

"Both. Clever girl. See, we knew you'd catch on."

Somehow it didn't sound like praise to me. Murtaugh looked at me with a face of stone, while the other man ignored us. He paced the length of the office again and again, smoked, looked out the windows, and never stopped playing with his gun.

"But wait," I said. "I still don't understand it all. Why was Alan so far behind? That wasn't just Vera."

"Nah. He kept making the building better, fancier, more beautiful, classier. Slowed things down real bad. I dunno. In his heart he was more like an artist than a businessman, I guess. He just didn't get it, how upset his partners were getting. Wouldn't listen."

"They killed him? To get him out of the way?" I tried to keep the outrage out of my voice. "Couldn't they just have bought him out? Or forced him out?"

"He wouldn't go," Murtaugh said simply. "And the legal route, suing or something, meant too much publicity. Now someone will take over who will listen to reason."

"You?"

"Me? Go on. I'm not an executive type. I'm just a workingman who does what he's told."

"You know who killed him, though, don't you?"

For the first time that day, I caught a flicker of expression.

"Was it you? You did that?" I felt my voice shake. "Of course. He opened the door to someone he knew—and trusted. Who worked for him. Who worked for his father."

Murtaugh's face went red, but he looked at me steadily as he said, "Not exactly."

"What?"

"Not exactly. I didn't exactly work for him."

I finally understood. "You worked for the men who had the money. You were—what?—keeping an eye on things? And when you worked for Stan too?"

"That's about it. I didn't work for Alan. You could say he worked for *me*, a I was representing my bosses." He looked away, off into a dark corner of the room, and added softly, "Don't think I was happy about it. I liked the guy. Knew him since he was a kid. Ate meals at his parents' home. But I didn't really have a choice. And I did it clean. He never knew."

"Poor Alan."

"Yeah, poor Alan. But he was a wimp, ya know. Couldn't turn down the dough, then couldn't do what he needed to. Couldn't even scare that Vera off."

"That was *Alan?*"

Murtaugh smiled slightly at my response. "He knew he needed to stop her, but he just couldn't go all the way with it. He was like a gentleman. He wanted to be a good guy, you know, *cultured*. Stan should've never sent him to Princeton."

"And you used Vera's gun."

"Yeah, the old two-birds-with-one-stone idea. I knew she had a gun. Matter of fact, that day we met at the site, you almost caught me putting it back."

The other man said, "You gonna spill your guts all afternoon?"

Murtaugh replied, "Don't you ever go to church? Confession is good for the soul." For just a second, I felt as if he meant it, but his next words were "Besides, it ain't going nowhere, any more than what you'd tell a priest. We'll finish this just as soon as it gets a little darker and Tommy comes back with the message about where they want it."

Keep them distracted, my mind screamed. Get them off guard. Ask another question. Any one would do.

"What really happened to Kevin Conley?"

"What really happened was an accident."

"But not just the one everyone thinks, I bet."

"No. Not exactly. Kevin was getting tight with your friend Vera, hanging around, helping her work. We used to kid him, that he was after her ass, but he said no, she was too old, he got plenty, and he was just interested in what she was doing. Then he started blabbering about how important this dig was and how he found something on his own that was gonna knock her socks off. That's just what he said, 'knock her socks off.' 'Put it on the map,' he said. Prove everything she thought. I never did find what it was, but once he was gone, no one else even knew about it.''

''Proof was the last thing you wanted, right?''

''Couldn't let it happen. If it did, it might mean even more delays, for who knew how long?''

''So?''

''He didn't know how I was thinking. We went out for a few beers, and he wanted me to come back there so he could show me what they were working on. He was going to show me everything, how they worked, what it all meant. Like a little kid with a new bike, that's what he was like. All excited because he was learning something new, and couldn't wait to tell everyone about it. Thought I would be excited too.'' He stopped, and then went on, explaining. ''We went back a long ways, me and his family. Thought of me kind of like one of his uncles.''

''So, you went back to the site with him that night?''

''Yeah. He was showing me how they scrape off the dirt and find little bits of things. Looked like junk to me, but he said it all means something.

Started talking about pirates, said there was something valuable they were gonna find, said he had definite proof. That's when I knew it was a problem, 'cause right at the beginning, Vera had a little meeting with some of us, told us what she hoped to find and what it would mean."

"What did you do?"

"I take Kevin aside and try to explain why it couldn't happen that way. I mean, I lay it on the line. Tell him to get rid of what he found and start trying to discourage Vera. Said it would be safer for her, too. Even offer him a chance to make some extra dough if he'd work with us on this."

He stopped again. I had to keep him going. "I bet he didn't take you up on it."

"Nope. He got mad. He just didn't, wouldn't, understand that it was better for Vera that way too. Safer. Better for everyone if we could get what we wanted, get her out fast, doing it easy and clean."

In spite of my own danger, I was fascinated. Like a mouse with a cobra. "Let me guess," I said softly. "Did you have a fight?"

"Yeah, finally. Kevin lost his temper, the goddamn fool, said he wouldn't let us do anything to hurt Vera, said he'd tell everyone. Finally took a swing at me, and I hit back. In the end, he hit his head."

"He was twenty years younger than you are, at least, and bigger, and he must have been in great shape from construction work. How could you stand up to him?"

"I had help." He looked off into that dark corner again and added softly, "Don't think I feel good about it. I still remember his face when he understood what I was asking him to do. Right until that minute he looked up to me. I wish I could've just convinced him. Or bribed him. Or beat some sense into him." He stopped talking abruptly.

Was there an opening here? A tiny weak spot? I said softly, "You didn't mean it to happen, did you?"

"That's what I'm saying. So we made it look like an accident."

"I know it was just business," I said, sounding as neutral as possible, "but I imagine it was still tough, two dead young men you've known all their lives. We talked that day after Alan— Remember? You weren't faking how you felt." He turned his face away from me, but I could see his skin redden, and a tremor in his jaw.

The other one, the one holding the gun, said, "She talks too much, Jerry. You want I should just shut her up?"

"And what difference does it make if she does talk? We got nothing else to do. You don't like it, you go out for a while."

"Leave you alone? Sure it's okay? I could go for a beer."

"Sure I'm sure. I can handle this one alone."

"Thanks. I owe you. Leave you this?" He held up the gun.

"Yeah, put it right here on the table. I wasn't carrying when I got called to deal with this. And bring me a cold one when you come back. Slice of pizza would be good, too."

The other man went out, and Murtaugh left the gun lying on the table near his hand. I wondered if I could make it to the door before he picked it up, and knew I could not.

I repeated sympathetically, "It must be tough on you. I think someone made you do some jobs you didn't really want to do."

"It's the truth," he said softly, almost to himself, not looking at me. "All these years, I've done whatever I was told to do; then they want this. They said it's just business, just like it always is. Just business."

"Killing a kid who you played with when he was a baby? Whose family you knew since *you* were a kid?"

"Kevin was an accident! I told you that. If only he hadn't of fought back so hard—"

"And Alan?"

"He gave me no choice! He couldn't do what had to be done. Lacked the balls. He had smarts, charm, education, but he just wasn't man enough.

His old man would've done it, back when he was still himself.''

"Done what?"

"Whatever. Sent in a crew in the middle of the night and bulldozed the damn hole in the ground, if he had to, and said it was all a misunderstanding later. Pay a fine, make nice to the powers, but in the meantime, it's too late, and the building goes up. But that was Stan in his prime, not Alan."

Most of the time he was talking to me, he wasn't really looking at me. He was staring off into the dark room. And I was staring at that gun. I wondered how much time I had before his partner returned.

Keep him talking, I thought. He's not really paying attention to me, and his guard is down. Maybe. And maybe I could get it lower. I'd better be able to call on twenty years of getting around people's guard today.

"Hard, isn't it," I said, "to have to do things you don't feel good about doing. I've had to do it myself sometimes. Deceive people, betray confidences, all that. I bet you'd rather just be a nice person, but the job says you can't. I've decided it's time to get out. Could you?"

"Get out? No chance. You don't just get a gold watch and retire to a Florida condo."

"What would you do if you could?" Keep distracting him, I thought. In a minute I would dive for the gun. It was my only chance. If I ran, I knew he'd shoot me.

"Just be a builder somewhere. Some little place. Upstate, maybe. Saratoga's nice. Build summer houses. Take in the races."

"Just be a citizen?"

"Yeah. I could deal with that. Sounded too ordinary when I was young and dumb. Why be Joe Citizen when I could be on the inside? Yeah, I could do it now. Take communion without expecting lightning to strike the church." He shook his head as if to clear it. "Jesus. I'm talking like an old woman." He put his hand out for the gun, reassuring himself. Reasserting himself. Too late now for me to get it.

I jumped. I threw myself as hard as I could at the table, forcing it away from him, turning it over, the gun sliding away. He jumped up shouting, grabbing, and just missing the gun.

There wasn't time to pick it up. The value of my surprise was measured in seconds, and he'd tackle me if I stopped. Much as I longed to pick it up, turn, and use it to stop him in his rush toward me, I couldn't. Without breaking my stride, I managed to kick it, hard. I heard it go skittering to the far end of the long, dark space, and I heard him curse.

I jerked the door open—stopped to see if I could lock it from the outside—no footsteps behind me— he must be looking for the gun—no lock, dammit!

I flew down the stairs with no plan except to run. Steps behind me now, but no one shooting. I burst through the door and looked frantically for cover. The next nearest door was padlocked, but there was another building just across the parking lot. Lots of doors. Loading bays. Places to hide.

I sprinted for it, panting and cursing myself for being in such rotten shape, but fear was moving me pretty well even if athletic conditioning couldn't. I had almost made it when a car came flying down the parking lot, spraying gravel. I could hear Murtaugh behind me. Now the other guy was jumping from the car and running too. They were coming from two sides; I'd be trapped between them in a minute.

When I darted left, changing directions in midstride, I threw them off just long enough to duck into the alley between two buildings. It bought me a moment, no more. I stood there gasping, knowing that one of them would be around to block the other end of the alley in a minute. I was trapped unless there was a way into one of the buildings.

There was no way. I looked toward the other end of the alley and saw that there might be just one other escape. The men hadn't found me yet, but they were near. I could hear them shouting, telling me I didn't have a chance; that I should come out; that they had a gun. They fired it once, just to prove it to me.

Get rid of my sandals. Rip off my long, clinging skirt. Take a deep breath and burst out of the shelter of the alley. I ran across the asphalt to the docks and didn't stop. Another deep breath, and I hit the water in a flat racing dive. I went under to the sounds of shouting and a gun, and swam underwater as long as my breath held out.

I didn't know where I was going. It'd been years since I swum regularly. The water was filthy. I was terrified to think about what might be in the water with me. Anything from typhoid germs to a corpse or two. But I wasn't as terrified of any of that as I was of the two men onshore.

When I put my head up just a bit for air, I heard a bullet, but saw that they were both still onshore. Maybe they couldn't swim? And I saw pilings in the water, not too far away, but around a curve. Not visible from where they stood? And a place to cling and hide? Now I had a direction.

It soon seemed as though I had misjudged the distance. Or perhaps the current was pulling me away. Each breath scraped the inside of my lungs. With each stroke my arms and legs grew heavier. It was almost too much effort to get my nose and mouth above water level for air. I remember thinking how unfair it was. I was going under, and I still hadn't met my mother.

When I finally felt hands pulling me out of the water, I couldn't tell whose they were. I didn't care.

NINETEEN

I WOKE UP IN A BED. It felt all wrong. It came to
me slowly that it wasn't my own bed. It hurt to
move my head. Something in my arm hurt too. I
opened my eyes with effort. IV needle in my arm.
Curtains next to my bed. It seemed I was in a hospital. I winced at the pain the sunlight caused my
eyes and head, and someone closed the blinds. I
had a sensation of sinking underwater.

The next time I opened my eyes, there was no
sun coming through the blinds. The room was almost dark, but I could see a warm circle of light
over there, in the corner. A lamp. A chair. Someone
in the chair. I had to close my eyes again.

The someone came to the bed and said softly,
"Are you awake, honey? Would you like something?"

I tried to speak. I wanted to ask questions, a lot
of questions, but I couldn't seem to get a sound out
of my throat.

"Water?" the voice asked.

I must have nodded, because there was a glass,
with a straw bent to reach my mouth, and an arm
across the back of my shoulders to help me lift my
head.

"Sip slowly."

I sipped and then lay back and fully opened my eyes at last. A woman stood beside me, her expression worried. She had bright green eye shadow, deep circles under her eyes, and red hair.

"Sally?" My voice croaked it out.

"Yes, dear. Hush now and rest."

And I did.

I woke up again with sun pouring through the venetian blinds, and I found I could keep my eyes open. I could turn my head. She was still there.

"Hello." My own voice startled me. It seemed I could speak again, just barely.

"Hello to you." She held a glass out to me, and I sipped the apple juice.

"Sally? Is it—that is—are you?"

"That's me, honey. I've been waiting right here until you woke up."

I tried to control the buzzing flies in my head long enough to have a focused thought.

"Why am I here? Am I in a hospital?"

"Yes, you are. Coney Island Hospital. You were pulled out of the water by a boater—you were one lucky girl—but you hit your head pretty bad."

I moved my hand to touch the part of my head that throbbed most, and winced.

"Yes, it hurts pretty bad, doesn't it? You're full of painkillers right now. And one of the shots those bastards fired at you did some damage here." She pointed to my aching shoulder. "It's just a flesh wound, though. Nothing long-term. And of course we pumped you full of antibiotics to protect you from all the junk in the harbor water."

"But," I said. "But—" I couldn't seem to quite formulate the thought I wanted. Or any thought. I tried again. "Me. How did they know I was me? Police? Ambulance?"

"Ah," she said. "Well, the police were already looking for you. I heard you call me, you know, when you were pushed into that car."

"I hollered. Sally."

"That's right. And you had another friend there, a Russian, ready to go after you himself, hijacking a cab, if necessary."

So Anatoly was there, looking after me. My friend.

"Go back to sleep now. You'll have plenty of time later to hear the rest and tell us the missing pieces. For now, just know you're safe and cared for."

My eyes closed again, against my will, and the next time I woke up, I found I could keep them open without effort. My head still hurt, but the pain had receded to a dull throb. If I didn't move, my shoulder wasn't too agonizing. There was an ugly bruise where the IV needle had been, but the needle was gone.

There was Sally, and with her, a large man in casual clothes.

"Peter?"

"Hey, kiddo. Are you back?"

"Guess so. I'm still a little confused. Can you tell me what happened?"

"Nope. I've been waiting for you to tell us. Are you up to making a statement?"

"Only if you tell me everything else after."

He grinned. "You're back, all right. Okay, let's get started."

When I was done, Peter said, not unkindly, "Do you think sometimes you're a little stupid? Not to mention you should've told me what you knew."

"I didn't know for sure what I knew." I ignored the remark about stupidity. I thought I'd be on shaky ground if I tried to deny it, so I changed the subject. "Did you ever find Vera?"

He shook his head. "Not yet."

"Now it's your turn. What happened to me?"

"Some boaters found you in the water and saw two men onshore shooting at you. They hauled you in and radioed for help. In the meantime, you had some friends who were already raising holy hell with the first patrol car they flagged down. I understand there were threats to steal the car and go after you themselves," he said dryly, with a glance at Sally. "So, by the time you were pulled out of the water, the department was already looking for you. Your Russian friend was pounding the desk about the Elkans, and that's how it got to me.''

"I learned a lot. Can you use it? I know it's hearsay. I have notes, too, from before, in my computer at work.''

"Kiddo, don't worry about it. We know exactly where they took you. The boaters saw them, so we went over the whole area pretty good. What do you think we found in that deserted old building? A nice little hiding place. We also found a purse full of your ID. And what else?''

I couldn't think. It all seemed too long ago, but Peter was grinning.

"You women carry the damnedest stuff in your bags. Wallet, keys, makeup, pens, checks. Credit cards. Notebook. Aspirin. Cookies. A whole store. And a tape recorder.''

"You don't mean it.''

"Yeah, I do. It's all there. Only thing we can't figure out is how you turned it on when they had a gun on you.''

I shook my head. Lightly. It still hurt. "I don't know. I didn't. It went on by accident, sometime when we were struggling, I guess. I can't believe it.''

"Believe it. When we find Murtaugh, and we intend to, his own words are gonna convict him.'' He leaned over to kiss me on the cheek. "I'll be back. Sweet dreams.''

"Sally?"

"Yes, dear?"

"Was Anatoly here? I have to thank him."

"He's been here every day, but he never caught you awake. However, *we* have become quite chummy."

"Every day? How many days has it been?"

"Four."

"Four?" I think I must have shouted it. "What's today?"

"Thursday. Thursday night."

Thursday.

"Omigod. There's someone coming to see me this weekend. He's probably been trying to get in touch with me. I've got to get my messages. Do I have a phone here?" I struggled to get up.

"Easy, easy! I'll get it for you."

"And pen and paper."

"Yes, yes, right here. Here, let me hold the phone for you."

I punched in the codes and got all my messages from work and home. And I finally knew where Vera was. And Tony had left several increasingly bewildered messages. He was still in Detroit, I believed and hoped, returning his children to their mother and waiting to hear from me.

Sally helped prop me up with pillows and deal with the complexities of a long-distance call from the hospital. Then she tactfully disappeared.

"Tony?"

"Kay? Where the hell have you been?" He sounded baffled, worried, annoyed, hurt. At the sound of his voice, tears of exhaustion, tension and fear, and relief began trickling from my closed eyes. I leaned back against the pillows and tried to find my voice.

The call didn't take long. He could tell I was exhausted and drugged, and said not to talk. He'd be there Saturday night, straight from the airport.

I fell back against the pillows, unable for a moment even to stretch out my arm to put the phone down.

Sally took it from me. "Someone special?"

"Yes. I guess so. Not sure."

"Hmm. Sounds interesting. Tell me in the morning?"

When the two dozen coral and apricot roses arrived next morning, Sally thought that was even more interesting, but when she asked me, I said firmly, "First, tell me about my father."

She almost dropped my breakfast tray. After she put it down with shaking hands, she sank into a seat herself and said, "What do you mean?"

I looked at her steadily. The bed rest and medication were finally working. I felt rested and clear-headed at last.

"I know, Sally. I knew when I sent you the note. I've been looking for you."

"But why? And how? I just don't understand."
Her complexion was suddenly pale under the
makeup. Even her hair color seemed dimmed.

"I was in Falls City this summer. Someone told
me I was adopted."

"Who? Your parents always wanted to keep it a
secret. No one knew."

"One person knew."

"That lawyer? Campbell?"

"Yes. He wanted to use it to bribe me. He would
tell me all about it if I'd back off on an ugly story
about his family."

Sally's face had a question, but I said only, "It's
a long story. I'll tell you sometime, not now. Anyway, I tracked down my birth certificate, my real
one, and figured it out. And I spent the last month
finding you."

She held my hand in a tight grip and said shakily,
"And almost died."

"Maybe," I said, "but because of my own stub-
bornness, not because I was looking for you."

"I'm glad you found me," she said, holding my
hand even tighter. "I stopped coming to visit when
you were little because that's what your parents
wanted. They were afraid of questions—and," she
added with the ghost of a grin, "they thought I was
a bad influence."

"Were you?"

"Maybe. I led a kind of wild life, by their Falls

City standards, anyway. I danced in Vegas for a while. Married three times. I like the horses and liked to live near the tracks. They could see where I was headed, I guess. Straight to hell, by their standards.''

She didn't sound as if she agreed with them, and I didn't either. I merely said, "Adventurous life. Please tell me.''

"Got a couple of days?''

"Well, yes!'' I smiled. "I understand I'll be right here.''

"I'll tell it to you in pieces, then. We have a long time to catch up and lots to tell. I know you have your own stories, too, and I want to hear them all. Every word. I'll start with your father. And then you need to sleep some more," she said sternly.

"Okay," she began. "I was seventeen, in nurses' training in Rome. New York, that is, not Italy. There was an air force base there.''

"I wonder if that was it? There was something on my birth certificate that said Rome. He was in the air force? Did he get shipped out? Korea, maybe? Too late for World War Two.''

She smiled. "Sounds like the Hollywood version. I hope you don't mean the one with the handsome pilot, the cruelly deceived, innocent young girl, and the tragic telegram from the War Department? You must've seen too many movies as a sweet young girl yourself. No, honey, the truth is—

well, I don't know if you'll think it's better or worse.

"I met him at a dance at the base, and I think we recognized each other right from the start. I was a young hell-raiser for sure, off my parents' leash for the very first time and hungry to try everything I could. Looking for trouble, and that's just what he was. And the most fun of any man I've ever met, and believe me, I've met plenty."

"What was he like?"

"Tall and dark-haired, like you. Not really handsome, but sexy? I couldn't sleep at night, thinking about him. He drove a car as if it was a plane, did parachute dropping for fun, jumped backward off the highest diving board. I was crazy for him."

"Were you in love with him?" I asked it seriously, and didn't think, until much later, that it was a sentimental question for a hardened old reporter.

Sally responded with a look half surprised, half cynical. "Kay, I was seventeen! What did I know about love, or anything else either? It was lust and adventure and, I don't know what, teenage high spirits, I guess. I wasn't his only girl, I did know that, and to tell the truth, I had a couple of other fellas on the string. He wasn't the first either, but it was a whole other thing when we were together. When he died, I was about as mad as I was grieving."

"He died? What happened? You said, not Korea."

"Car accident. He was drunk. Stupid, isn't it? Probably thought he was in a plane and could just fly over the other car. I found out I was pregnant with you a week later."

"Jesus."

"Oh, yes. I managed to finish the year at school and went home, and my folks pretty much threw me out onto the streets. That's when my big sister, your mom, stepped in. She told the neighbors she was pregnant after years of trying, very high risk, had to be under doctors' care in Rome the whole time. And off we went. She found a place to stay, doctors, everything. She stood by me the whole time, right in the teeth of our parents calling me a tramp and swearing they'd never speak to me again. I made that part easy—I never spoke to them. After that, I owed her everything."

"It's hard to imagine Mom with so much spunk. And planning it all out."

Sally smiled ruefully. "Probably the one little spark of rebellion in her whole conventional little life." She fussed over my covers and pillow and dimmed the light, saying, "I did finally finish nursing school, and I'm on duty now. It's time for you to rest."

I went to sleep, but as I was drifting off, I heard her whisper, "I wanted you back, all those years, but the adoption was final. I knew she'd never give you up. She'd give me up first. And she did, for a long time.''

We spent the next two days catching up. She'd had three worthless husbands, lived both high and rough. She told me all that had led up to her life now, as a nurse-companion to a kind and wealthy old man she'd met years ago at Hialeah. Her stories were colorful and complicated, and she laughed a lot. She made the hard parts sound like adventures, and claimed to regret nothing.

"It's been a hell of a life, honey. Met all kinds of people. Been everywhere. It's the life I must have wanted, 'cause I sure did go after it. The only regret is that I never could have any more children. That's a kick in the pants from fate, isn't it? Hell, it hasn't always been easy or fun, but what if I'd stayed in Falls City? Lived your mom's life? Forty years with the same house, same job? Same *man?*'' She shuddered. "Sometime I'll tell you about the famous movie star I dated in Vegas. And my second husband, the jockey. Now, he had some life. Oh, no, honey, no regrets.''

The stories and laughter didn't disguise the fact that some of it had been hard. She was a survivor. And at last I knew where my craving for adventure had come from, and my need to tell stories, too.

Anatoly came to see me several times, each time with smuggled food. He was positively triumphant the time he sneaked in a whole pizza. He called me stubborn, played down his role in my rescue, and said he'd kill me himself if I ever did anything so stupid again. His wife punched him lightly on the arm and ordered him to leave me alone. "Hush, Anatoly!" She said to me, "He was worried. You must forgive."

Vera called twice a day, a free woman. She insisted on cleaning my apartment for me, and stocking my refrigerator, to get it ready for my return. In response to my skepticism, she swore with great dignity that she did so know how to clean and grocery shop, she just didn't choose to do it much. Then she said softly, "Let me help you somehow, Kay. I owe you."

And on Saturday, at dinnertime, Tony walked in, carrying his luggage, straight from the airport as promised. Sally was there; she looked him over briefly and then disappeared.

He sat on the side of the bed and held my hand, and kissed me and kissed me. He never moved while dusk crept into the room, and I told him everything about the last few weeks. Almost everything. I knew the moment he walked in how little Alan had really meant to me. I didn't need to tell Tony about it.

When the nurses shooed him out, he promised to come back in the morning with a car to take me home.

Sally returned and said, far too innocently, "Nice-looking young man."

By then I was starting to know her. I laughed and said, "You're dying to know."

"Of course I am. Is he the fellow you were so anxious to call?"

"Yes."

"And what is he to you?"

"I don't know. I just really don't know. He lives in Falls City." I saw her startled look. "Yes, it's another story. And I'm here. And he—he scares me. I like him too much. *That* scares me."

"Is he a good man?"

"Yes, I think he really is."

"Makes you laugh? Plenty to talk about?"

"Yes."

"Feels right in bed?"

"Yes. Definitely."

"Well, honey, you're thirty-eight years old. If you don't know enough to grab something good by now, I sure don't know if you'll know enough to listen to a little motherly advice. And I haven't been enough of a mother to expect you to, either. However, that isn't going to stop me. This is it: What are you waiting for?"

I didn't have an answer for that. Maybe it was time to stop waiting.

EPILOGUE

ONE MONTH LATER, I watched two enormous men load my furniture and crated possessions onto a moving van. That night, Tony would supervise the unloading at the house I had rented in Falls City, and I would be on a plane the next day. A full carton of research on small-town life went on the truck, but no contract for the book I wanted to write. I didn't care anymore. I had some money saved, a pension plan to borrow from, a promise of freelance work if I needed it. I'd manage.

The last few weeks had been a blur of paperwork, address changes, and farewells. Vera had treated me to a champagne-soaked dinner, promised to visit, and elatedly conveyed the news that the dig would continue. The disarray in Elkan's company put the whole building project on hold; there was no one now to object to her continuing work. And the public interest in her findings had, perhaps, influenced the relevant city offices to mandate a delay in the building in any case. The results of the work promised to be all she had hoped for and more.

The Sorkins had taken me to a Russian nightclub for what Anatoly promised would be a "a wild night, Russian style." Anatoly had scrutinized

Tony with great suspicion on his visits to New York, but when our last evening together ended at 3:00 a.m., he whispered, "Tony is good man. Hang on to him."

My colleagues threw me a party one night after work. Half of them predicted moss would grow on my brain and I'd be back in New York in a month, screaming for polluted air to breathe. The other half were openly, sometimes nakedly, envious.

Only one concern had made me keep hesitating, changing my mind again and again, even as I filled out address-change cards. It was not my colleagues' skepticism; my own cold feet at leaving the career that had been my life for twenty years; my fear of being too involved with Tony. It was leaving my mother so soon after I had found her.

In that month we'd begun to know each other. She introduced me to her frail, sweet, elderly employer, and I introduced her to Vera and, by phone, to Marsha in Miami. We'd learned that our life experiences, our interests, and our styles were worlds apart. Galaxies apart. And yet I kept finding myself in her, in an attitude, a chance expression, a tone of voice, a joke. It was an exciting, unnerving experience, seeing myself reflected back to me by someone else. And it was a completely new one.

Finally she said to me, "Honey, there's no way we'll lose each other now. They've got phone service up there in the North Country. Planes fly. I hear there's an interstate that goes right through to the Canadian border. I haven't been there in thirty years. Maybe it's time for me to deal with a few ghosts, just like it's time for you to make a break from your old life. You wouldn't wiffle-waffle like this if you were going after a story, I bet!" I had to admit that was true. "So, now it's time to go after your life instead."

The next day I turned in my resignation at the magazine. I just had one last story to write. I didn't learn until after it was published that they found Jerry Murtaugh's body in the water under the Verrazano-Narrows Bridge, with a bullet in his head.

The story began:

In a city that changes constantly, some things never change. In a city built on an island, land is more scarce than money, land is more valuable than money, land is more valuable than lives. This is the story of a piece of land, and money, and death. The first two deaths are mysteries not yet solved, and they took place centuries ago, when Dutch was still commonly heard on the streets of a city recently called New Amsterdam. The last two took place this summer, and they are no longer mysteries.

The
AUDUBON
Quartet
RAY SIPHERD

A Jonathan Wilder Mystery

Artist and bird lover Jonathan Wilder is eager to view four newly discovered works of legendary painter John James Audubon, purchased by friend and art philanthropist Brian Ravener. But at the first showing, notorious art critic Abel Lasher declares the Audubon Quartet to be fakes.

Hours later, Lasher is found murdered and Ravener is arrested. Anxious to help his friend, Wilder dives into the world of high art, where powerful collectors play for high stakes.....

Available May 1999 at your favorite retail outlet.

Take 2 books and a surprise gift FREE!

SPECIAL LIMITED-TIME OFFER

Mail to: The Mystery Library™
3010 Walden Ave.
P.O. Box 1867
Buffalo, N.Y. 14240-1867

YES! Please send me **2 free books** from the Mystery Library™ and my free surprise gift. Then send me 3 mystery books, first time in paperback, every month. Bill me only $4.19 per book plus 25¢ delivery and applicable sales tax, if any*. There is no minimum number of books I must purchase. I can always return a shipment at your expense and cancel my subscription. Even if I never buy another book from the Mystery Library™, **the 2 free books and surprise gift are mine to keep forever.**

415 WEN CJQN

Name   (PLEASE PRINT)

Address   Apt. No.

City   State   Zip

MYS98

MIND GAMES

C.J. KOEHLER

A RAY KOEPP MYSTERY

Searching for a killer's motivation requires logic and insight into human nature, skills at which former priest Ray Koepp excels.

The victim is Isaac Steiner, a prominent man in academic circles and founder of Friar's Close, a housing community conceived as a refuge from urban violence.

As Koepp begins to investigate, he confronts the myriad sides of human nature, and discovers life at Friar's Close is far from idyllic.

Available May 1999 at your favorite retail outlet.

PATRICIA TICHENOR WESTFALL

A MOLLY WEST MYSTERY

MOTHER OF THE BRIDE

Even a seasoned list maker like Molly West can get the jitters, especially when her daughter announces she's getting married in two months—and worse, that the wedding will be a Civil War reenactment.

Then a bridesmaid finds a skeleton in a cave where escaped slaves used to hide on the Underground Railroad. But clearly the human remains aren't that old. And as Molly starts digging, she discovers something old…something new…and something very deadly.

Available May 1999 at your favorite retail outlet.

A DOUBLE COFFIN

GWENDOLINE BUTLER

A COMMANDER JOHN COFFIN MYSTERY

Former British Prime Minister Richard Lavender still knows when things need handling quickly and discreetly. Lavender's father was a serial killer. And the ex-PM wants to put matters right, nearly three-quarters of a century later. Hence the summons to Commander John Coffin of London's Second City police.

But when a journalist investigating Lavender is murdered, past and present collide, proving what Coffin already knows: that the past never disappears—it's buried, only to resurface in shocking and menacing ways.

Available May 1999 at your favorite retail outlet.